adoring ALEJANDRO

FALLING DOWN #3

EVE BLACK

Copyright © 2022 by Danica Sorber (w/a Eve Black)

Adoring Alejandro—Falling Down #3

All rights reserved. No part of this publication may be reproduced, distributed, or transmitted in any form or by any means, including photocopying, recording, or other electronic or mechanical methods, without the prior written permission of the publisher, except in the case of brief quotations embodied in critical reviews and certain other noncommercial uses permitted by copyright law.

This book is a work of fiction. All names, characters, locations, and incidents are products of the authors' imaginations. Any resemblance to actual persons, things, living or dead, locales, or events is entirely coincidental.

Editor/Proofreader: Wordsmith Alchemy Author Services
Cover Designer: Angela Haddon/Angela Haddon Book Cover Design
Formatting: Stacey Blake/Champagne Book Design

*For the ones who love from afar, watching longingly,
wishing that **they** would finally see you.*

playlist

"Say Something"—Justin Timberlake ft. Chris Stapleton

"Valio la Pena"—Marc Anthony

"Feeling Exactly"—Bass Astral x Igo

"Dancing in the Dark"—Bass Astral x Igo ft. Runforrest

"Watermelon Sugar"—Harry Styles

"For the Now"—Kovich ft. Annie Bosko

"Lonely"—Nathan Wagner

"Suffocate"—Nathan Wagner

adoring ALEJANDRO

prologue

Mendez Family Cemetery
Natchez, Mexico
Seven years ago

Alejandro Dupree stood over the yawning pit in the earth, glaring down at the shiny black coffin, its surface blanketed with long stem roses in white. As though the flora themselves were grieving for the one sleeping inside.

His mother loved white roses. Said they were pure, like they'd been untouched by the pollution of the world. Pollution of men and their deeds.

Men like his father.

The hand woven with his squeezed his fingers, and he turned to look at the only person in the world he loved more than himself. His little sister, Sallina, offered him a broken smile, her green eyes faded with grief.

"Do you think she's happier now?" she asked, her voice reedy. At nineteen, Sally was still just discovering life outside of Maison Enchante´, the massive, cold southern plantation house in Savannah, Georgia, that was more like a mausoleum for the dead, than a home for the living.

"Honestly, I hope so." Some of his earliest memories of his mother were of her singing Mexican lullabies, rocking him to sleep, and telling him stories of when she was young. Those were the good memories. The memories he would hold on to forever. Those were stories he would tell his children about their *abuela*.

It was the *other* memories, though, the ones that made his stomach twist and the bile rise that he would scour from his mind forever. If that were possible.

"I hope that, wherever she is, she is much happier than she ever was here."

Sally sniffled, pressing a balled-up tissue under her nose. Of the both of them, Sally was the most affected by their mother's death. She'd lived in Maison Enchante´ during the worst years, when their father fucked anything that moved, and their mother drank anything that could numb the pain. Sally had seen it all. After AJ left for Miami at eighteen, it had been Sally and Mama against the Monster. Sally took upon herself the responsibility of making sure their mother ate, that she didn't drown in her vomit, and that she looked presentable when *he* hosted house parties. Year after year, more pieces of their mother died. And Sally watched it happen, had seen their mother's decline, had heard her crying out alone in her room, had witnessed their father parading women through the house—even fucking them out in the open for their mother and Sally to see.

Sally didn't know that AJ knew. She loved him, had tried to hide the worst of it from him, but he knew it all.

Before he'd escaped, he'd asked their housekeeper, Lisana, to keep an eye on his sister. Lisana had worked for the family since before he was born, and she was loyal to their mother and her children. She'd agreed to watch over Sally and keep AJ informed about the goings-on in the house. So, there was little he didn't know about the horrors that Sally and their mother had faced.

And AJ had been forced to do nothing. His asshole father effectively tying his hands, threatening to ruin everything AJ was trying to build.

Their father hadn't even bothered attending his own wife's funeral, having dropped the façade of adoring husband years ago. Everyone knew he was cheating on her, flashing his mistresses all over, throwing his infidelities in her face. He never hid who he was—not like that first year when he was acting the dutiful husband…because he was waiting to get his hands on her dowry. The company her father, their maternal grandfather, had built with his own two hands. Once that first obligatory year was over, the true Henri Dupree was revealed for all to see. And he'd gloated in his victory.

The fucking bastard.

"I hate him, AJ! I hate him so much! I can't stand being his daughter," Sally hissed, her body vibrating with unspent rage. A rage he knew just as intimately as she did.

"I know, sis." And did he. As the eldest child and only son of Henri Dupree, AJ had known his fair share of pain—physical, emotional, and mental. Out of all of those, though, the mental anguish was the worst. He was never good enough for his father, never the son he wanted even though he was the son he was given. AJ didn't choose to be sired by that man, he didn't choose to be born into a family where imperfection wasn't tolerated. He didn't choose to be the son of a man who knew nothing of loyalty, faithfulness, compassion, or basic human dignity.

Their father was a monster. A monster who killed their mother.

"I have an idea," Sally broke through his thoughts, her smile now genuine.

"Oh? What's that? Skip the reception at the *hacienda* and catch a flight home tonight?"

Because their mother was born and raised in Natchez, she'd asked that her body be buried in the family cemetery, where she could be with her beloved mother and father again. Their great-uncle and his wife had planned a beautiful service and insisted on hosting the reception in their home for those who knew and loved their mother. There were few non-family members in attendance, but most of the people at the graveside service had known her when she was young…before their father got his hands on her. Corrupting her beauty, her innocence, and her heart.

Sally shook her head, her eyes bright. "No. We should change our name."

He furrowed his brow, confused. "What?"

"Henri Dupree should be cast out and burned to death, but sense we cannot remove him from our blood, we should be able to remove him from our mouths. Every time I have to introduce myself or write my name, he is there. Dupree."

AJ nodded, grinning. "You've got a point. So what should we change it to?"

Sally dropped her head, her lips trembling. "Mendez. We will take Mama's name. She was the last of her family, and we are the last of hers. We should carry her name."

Stunned by the conviction in his sister's voice, AJ swallowed a ball of tears. Damn, but she'd grown from the quiet, withdrawn, easily frightened girl she'd been three years ago, before she'd escaped.

Unable to speak for the tightness in his throat, he simply nodded.

"Yeah? That's a good idea, right?"

He swallowed again, and attempted a smile. "Good idea."

"So, from now on we're Mendezes."

"Yes. Dupree is dead."

As the gravesite cleared of mourners cloaked in black, Sally and AJ remained, standing solemnly and silently.

AJ couldn't shake the image of his mother, smiling at him, loving on him. That was the woman he wanted to remember, not the shell of a wife who finally crumbled, finding her end in pills and booze.

Lisana had found her. She'd left no note. No goodbye. And her children grieved for her, raged for her. But neither AJ nor Sally could understand why, if she was so miserable, she hadn't just left. AJ would have welcomed her to Miami with open arms. He would have taken care of her, helping her get back on her feet. He loved her. She was his mother.

So why, in the end, had she chosen to die rather than to live?

Love. For whatever fucked up reason, his mother loved his father. And it had killed her.

"What are you thinking about so hard over there?" Sally asked, interrupting his thoughts.

"I just don't understand why she stayed even after you left. I figured that she was there because he wouldn't let *you* leave, and she didn't want to abandon you to him. But even after you moved to Miami with me, she was there, taking his abuse, having his mistresses thrown in her face."

"Honestly, I think she spent most of the time drunk. When she wasn't drunk, she was sleeping. And…well, as horrible as it sounds, she actually loved him."

"He ruined her!"

"Yeah, but before that he was the charming older man who'd made promises of a beautiful life and family. She was too young and sheltered to realize she was being manipulated by a pro. He was handsome, said all the right things, and she fell hard."

"But once she saw him for who he truly was—"

"She still loved him. That was Mama, though. She loved deeply. It didn't matter that her husband was a cheating asshole, it mattered that she was in love with him, no matter how much it hurt. That's why she drank. The pain. She couldn't stop loving him even when she wanted to hate him."

"He didn't deserve a woman like Mama."

"No, he didn't."

"The sad part is, she could have actually found someone who would've loved her just as deeply, but she fell for *him* instead." AJ wanted to scream at the unfairness of it all.

"We can't change the past, AJ, as much as I wish we could…." AJ watched his sister's face, noting her expression. The way her eyes grew hazy, the way her jaw muscles tightened. She was slipping into memories.

"No, we cannot change the past," he agreed, and Sally

blinked, lifting her face to look at him again, her memories once again hidden. "But we can change what we will do in the future."

"What do you mean?" Sally tipped her head quizzically before meeting his gaze, her eyes beginning to brighten. Warmth spilled through his chest. He wanted this for his sister—this hope of happiness.

You deserve that, too.

"I mean that…I want to find a woman who will love me as deeply as Mama loved him. And when I find her, I will be everything our father wasn't. I will cherish her, adore her, and treat her like a goddamned queen."

"That's great and all, but what if you don't find someone like that? This world is full of posers who act one way but are really another."

They knew that from experience—their father being the biggest poser there was.

"I don't know exactly, I just know that I won't settle for just anyone. She has to be special."

"How will you know, though?"

"I just will." He grinned at Sally, his heart suddenly lighter than it had been in years. He dragged in a deep breath, closed his eyes, and said, "My heart will know her when I see her."

From the Desk of AJ Mendez

November 17th

My Swan, I know that by now you're probably annoyed with all the questions about who you are on the other side of the computer screen. But you have to know that I am desperate to know anything about you. I know your favorite color, but I don't know the color of your eyes. I know your favorite TV show, but I don't know what your face looks like when you laugh. I know you like 80s music cranked up high, but I don't know what it feels like to dance with you in my arms.

I need to meet you, my Swan. It's a hunger unlike anything I have ever felt before. You have to put me out of my misery. Just one single hint. Just one detail about you that I can use to help picture your face when I'm fucking my hand at night....

Okay, enough of my desperation.

So, in your last email you asked me what my favorite treat is. Well, when I was a kid, my housekeeper/second mom, Lisana, made these delicious, melt-in-your-mouth triple chocolate chip cookies. I can't tell you how many times I begged her to make them, and then snuck handfuls of them when she wasn't looking. LOL.

If I were answering you, face to face, I'd tell you that the best thing I've ever tasted is your lips.

Wishing for more,
AJ

chapter ONE

Harris Construction, LLC.
Jackson Key, FL
Present Day

MAEVE THOMAS SAT IN HER OFFICE, AT HER DESK, hunched behind her computer monitor, listening intently to a conversation she shouldn't. It wasn't the first time and definitely wouldn't be the last time she eavesdropped on her bosses as they chatted like the best friends and business partners they were. Then again, was it eavesdropping if they were holding their conversation right in front of her office door? The door open, their voices loud, carrying easily across the immaculate space? It was like they were asking her to listen in—and sometimes, they'd include her. When they even remembered she was there. Which was only when their conversation—or rather argument—needed an outside opinion.

"I can't believe you're actually eating those," her boss, Blaze Harris, said incredulously, his thick arms crossed over his even thicker, harder chest. The man was well made, sexy as all get out, and 100% in love with his girlfriend, the sweet yet sassy Anna. Watching those two together was like watching soft-core porn; sexy kisses, sensual touches, lots of murmured words, neck nuzzling…. It absolutely did *not* make Maeve jealous. Nope.

It did *not* make sad, shy, invisible Maeve want a romance and HEA of her own.

Her gaze flicked from Blaze to the other man standing just outside her office door.

Alejandro Mendez.

She heaved a wistful sigh. Yeah, she was a flipping liar. She *did* want all that—the sexy kisses, sensual touches, neck nuzzling and whispered words of love and seduction. She wanted all those things with her *other* boss, her sexy as hell, walking sex, perfect male specimen boss…who looked right through her.

"Of course, I'm going to eat them! They're my favorite," AJ replied around a mouthful of triple chocolate chip cookie.

Blaze snorted, rolling his eyes. "That isn't the problem, man, the problem is that you're trusting that whoever this chick is, she isn't trying to poison you. How can you trust that she didn't do something to them?"

Good question, Maeve pondered. For all AJ knew, those cookies were yummy with a dash of rat poison. Then again,

Maeve knew exactly what was in those cookies: chocolate chunks, flour, sugar, eggs…and love. Lots and lots of love.

It had taken her three tries to get them just right, based on the recipe he said his second "mom", Lisana, used to create the treats back when he was a little boy.

But neither Blaze nor AJ knew that. Or would ever know.

A sharp pang rattled through her chest at that thought. For all she felt for AJ, he would never feel the same for her. The real her. Maeve Thomas, Office Manager.

He was crushing on someone else. An anonymous online femme fatale. A woman he'd been chatting with for three months over email. The woman he'd been chatting with was witty, brash, bold, intelligent, and sassy—all the things AJ liked. She was a woman so amazing and wonderful, AJ couldn't help but fall for her.

She was Swan. A totally made up person.

Who also happened to be *her*. Maeve Thomas. Anonymously. Because she was an idiot who thought telling him she was crushing on him without telling him who she really was, was a good idea. So…maybe she wasn't *totally* made up, because Maeve was real, she really said and thought all the things she shared with AJ, she just felt more comfortable being that woman when AJ didn't know what she looked like.

In real life, out from behind the computer screen, AJ looked right through her. Sure, he smiled at her when he greeted her every morning, or when he asked her a question about this document or that file, but he never stopped to speak to her unless it was about business. To AJ Mendez, Maeve might as well be an office appliance.

For her, though, it had been love at first sight. Because life was a bitch like that.

adoring ALEJANDRO

Groaning at the ridiculous situation she'd gotten herself in, Maeve fought the urge to bang her head against her desk because, not only would that draw the attention of her bosses, it would also make her headache that much worse.

AJ finished chewing, his expression pensive. Finally, he replied, "I don't know how to explain it. Yeah, in the beginning I was skeptical—I mean catfishing is slimy as fuck, but…well, she never gave me that vibe, ya know. From that first email, all I ever felt was intrigued, like I wanted to know more about her. And the more we got to know each other, the more I got to know her, the more I…I don't know… trusted her, I guess."

Blaze stared at AJ, his lips thin. "But how do you know you can trust her?"

AJ shrugged. "I just do."

"You don't even know if she is real, she could be someone playing someone else. Hell, those cookies can be store bought and repackaged to make you think she actually made them."

Uh, that's a no. I definitely spent days working on the perfect recipe, and another couple of hours making that batch. And… she may or may not have eaten a batch or two on her own.

Her gaze moved from AJ to Blaze and then back to AJ, her mouth opening and closing as the urge to interrupt, to interject, to finally be seen flooded her throat. But she pushed it down, panic rising in its place.

No, she couldn't tell him anything, no matter how much she wanted to. The second AJ realized she was the one who'd been sending emails and treats, he'd fire her. Never mind the fact that he'd also probably look at her like she was a scheming bitch, using her wiles to trick him into falling for a fat, ugly nobody.

Nausea swirled in her belly, making her swallow.

EVE BLACK

She needed to get out of there—but AJ and Blaze were in the way.

Screw this!

Rising to her feet, Maeve smoothed her shaking hands down her boxy, beige skirt, and straightened her shoulders. Putting one foot in front of the other, she moved toward the door, praying the two men would ignore her as she slipped passed them and down the hallway to the bathroom…where she could puke in private.

Right before she could make a break for it, AJ's phone rang. Shoving the box of cookies under one arm, he used his other hand to retrieve his cell from the back pocket of his well-worn, ass hugging jeans.

Lord, to be that phone….

AJ peered down at the display and grunted, rolling his eyes.

"What?" Blaze asked, just as curious as Maeve about who called.

AJ grunted again, silencing the phone, and shoving it in his front pocket this time.

"That IT chick from White," AJ answered.

"Denise Walters?" Blaze asked, his eyebrows shooting north. "What's she calling you about?"

AJ sighed, pushing his long, fingers through the already mussed, dark brown locks. Sheared on the sides and left longer on the top, the dark curls made him look both sexy and adorable at the same time. What she would give just to feel the softness of his hair shifting between her fingers.

"She's been calling and texting like crazy the last two weeks."

"Why? You hit that?" Maeve cringed at Blaze's inquiry, wanting to know, and not wanting to know. It was a diabolical conundrum. Maeve wasn't an idiot, she knew AJ was a sexually active, red-blooded, American male, that with his looks, charm, and alpha tendencies, he was a goddamn catch. She also knew he was one of the sweetest, most thoughtful, and most compassionate man she'd ever known. Not that he showed that side of himself to anyone but his closet friends. She just wished she could be counted among them...out in the open.

She also wished he could be all hers. She didn't want to share him with any other woman, especially women like Denise Walters.

"Definitely haven't touched that. We met up when I was Miami last month to deal with the Hanger's Cove documents Sly was adamant needed to be completed that week, in Miami, with that group of ass kissers. Denise was there, chatted me up, invited me out. I took a raincheck. Since then, though, she's been blowing me up, texting about getting together when I'm back in Miami—and she even mentioned driving here to spend the weekend."

"The fuck?" Blaze barked, dropping his arms to tense up. "Like, she invited *herself* to spend the weekend with you?"

"Yup."

Maeve's gaze bounced from one man to the other, the urge to vomit slowly receding—until AJ's gaze landed on her...where she was standing...in the doorway...obviously eavesdropping on their conversation.

Ah, damn! What the hell is wrong with me? All she had to do was slip by them and go about her business. Instead, she'd gotten caught up in their back and forth, forgetting that she wasn't *actually* invisible.

"Maeve?" AJ said, his brow furrowing. "Where'd you come from?"

EVE BLACK

Ignoring the sharp jab in her chest at his question—because he obviously hadn't even considered she'd be there, in her own office—she mentally answered.

My mother. Venus. The dimension where they birth awkward nobodies from green pods.

"You are having a full-on conversation right in front of my office," she replied instead, grateful that her voice was steady and as neutral as she could make it while her heart was thundering in her throat. "I couldn't help but overhear. It wasn't like you two were whispering, either."

AJ grinned, his perfect smile transforming the furrow in his brow into a look of sheepish humor.

"Yeah, you're right. Sorry 'bout that. Hey, you want a cookie? They're the best thing I've ever put in my mouth." The man wiggled his eyebrows suggestively, a playful smirk on his face.

Blaze choked on a laugh, and Maeve could feel heat rise into her cheeks.

I bet I have something better for you to eat. Shit, her inner vixen was a filthy bitch!

Simultaneous images popped into her head. AJ eating her cookies while moaning about how good they tasted, and AJ eating her *"cookies"* while *she* was moaning about how good he was with his tongue.

Even greater heat bloomed in her core, spreading out over her sensitive flesh to burn her thoughts to ash.

Mumbling something about needing to poop—yes! She said *poop!*—she hurried past the men standing there staring at her with shocked expressions, and banged the employee's bathroom door shut behind her.

Face on fire, heart pounding, shame coursing through

her, Maeve sat on the closed toilet, bent over her knees, and begged for the floor to open up and swallow her.

In the fifteen minutes it took her to "poop", Maeve calmed her freak out, splashed some water on her face, and squared her shoulders. No, she wasn't a badass boss bitch who could face down her two sexy male bosses without stuttering out an embarrassing apology, but she was awkward and cowardly enough to slink back into her office, shut the door, and pretend it didn't happen at all.

It wasn't like Blaze cared about her weirdness—as long as she did her job. And it wasn't as though AJ would even remember her existence once she was out of sight.

Out of sight, out of mind.

God…that phrase had never been as heart crushing as it was in that moment.

Sure, online, she was a sassy, sensual sex kitten that AJ couldn't get enough of, but in real life, she might as well be the HAVE A GOOD DAY cat poster everyone walked right past. They give it a first look to see if it was important, then ignored it because it wasn't. Not to them.

Thankfully, she made it to her desk without seeing anyone, which wasn't really all the difficult since, besides her and Blaze and AJ, there were only two other employees that worked out of the office regularly. She checked the clock on her computer and sighed. It was lunchtime, which explained the echoing office, and the growling ache in her stomach.

Using the newly installed time keeping software on her computer to clock out for lunch, Maeve settled in at her desk for a cold ham and cheese, and an episode of Father Brown from the BBC America streaming website.

As an American, she should be slightly ashamed of her British tv show addiction, but she wasn't. BBC shows like

Father Brown, Sherlock, and Doctor Who were pure escapism. And with as much crap as she had in her life, she needed an escape every once in a while. Okay—every day. She watched them every day. And she was getting pretty good at emulating the accent, too.

She smirked to herself before taking a bite of her sandwich and hitting play.

The clock on her desktop blinked to 5:00 P.M. Another work day complete. While she couldn't say the day was without its mishaps—she said *poop!*—she was relieved she didn't have to see AJ again.

Standing to gather her things, she jumped and squeaked with a knock sounded at her office door.

"Maeve?" an all too familiar, sexy, unwelcome voice called out. "You okay in there?"

Aw, hell. No, she was not. Not anymore.

But she couldn't just ignore him when he knew she was in there and she would have to get by him to go home. While the urge to sit in silence and hope he went away was there, she knew it was about as ridiculous as all her other ideas had been lately.

Like playing the virtual vixen to a sex god.

"Yes!" she called out. "One second." She used the next *sixty* seconds to get her heartrate under control and straighten out her already immaculate desk.

Finally, she opened her door and nearly melted into a pool of lust.

AJ was standing there, hands shoved into his front pockets, his head hanging down but his gaze looking up at her through the fan of his long, thick, black eyelashes.

Tha-thump. This is what spontaneous human combustion feels like, isn't it?

adoring **ALEJANDRO**

"Hey, I heard Sally say you were meeting her and Anna at Happy Jack's," he remarked, a slight smile curving his luscious, beautiful lips. His five o'clock shadow framed his square jaw, emphasizing just how rugged he was. His nose, long, straight, and a little pointy at the end, added a regality to his face she couldn't help but want to worship. She wanted to cup his face in her hands…then rub her face against his like a cat in heat—purring and everything!

Maeve coughed, well aware that she probably looked like a dying fish with her too wide eyes and open mouth.

Get it together, woman!

She coughed again, blinked, and nodded. "Y-yes, I am. She's really nice, and Anna is, too. They've invited me to hang out a few times." Thinking about the vibrant and incredible women, Maeve smiled.

His gaze dropping to her mouth for a millisecond, his eyes darkened before lifting to meet hers again. This time, his smile was all types of wicked. Full on, melt-a-woman's-panties hawt. And it was directed at her.

Whaaaaat was that?

He chuckled, probably at the shocked confusion on her face. "I'm glad to hear that. Those two are great, though they might get you into trouble once or twice."

Maeve snorted, desperately pushing aside the need to fan her cheeks. "Who's to say they haven't done that already?"

AJ's green eyes widened in surprise, as though he couldn't quite believe dull as paper Maeve could do something bad.

Ugh, if he only knew!

"Oh yeah?" he asked, interest in his voice. "I've got to hear about this."

What? Why would he care—and why had he knocked on her door?

"Did you knock on my door to ask me about drinks with your sister?" Because, really, that made no sense.

AJ's mouth pinched. Raising one hand to rub at the delicious stumble on his chin, his smile was cockeyed.

"Um…actually, I wanted to apologize for earlier."

Blink.

"What?"

He cleared his throat and grabbed the back of his neck. Was AJ Mendez…nervous?

Oh boy.

"For what I said earlier…about the cookies…and the thing about my mouth. It was inappropriate to tease you like that. I know I might come across like a callous playboy, but I know better than to bring that shit into the office. I didn't mean to offend you with my remark, and I hope that you can forgive me and, hopefully, forget it ever happened."

Whoa.

She didn't even know what to say.

Drawing on the dregs of her bravery, she replied, "Forgiven and forgotten. Don't worry, I knew you were just playing around. No harm done. Seriously."

I know you would never be serious about a comment like that toward someone like me. Her "cookies" were safe from him, because he didn't want Maeve's cookies, he wanted Swan's.

Swallowing down the hurt she'd caused her own damn self with her own damn thoughts, Maeve offered AJ a quick smile, grabbed her purse off her desk, and left AJ standing in her office doorway. Staring at her back.

adoring **ALEJANDRO**

From the Desk of UNKNOWN SENDER

September 29th

Good morning.

No. You don't know me, but I know you. Yes, I know that sounds like I'm some sort of creepy stalker, but I'm not. I swear. More secret admirer than serial killer, I promise.

The truth…. I saw you. I fell in love with you. Crazy fairytale stuff, right? But it wasn't. For me, it was like being shot with Cupid's arrow, struck by lightning, hit by a truck, slapped in the face—they all sound painful, yes, but that's what it felt like to see you and then to suddenly know you were it for me.

I don't know what it was about you that hit me so hard. Yes, you're gorgeous as hell, but it wasn't just that. You carried yourself with this confidence, purpose, and strength that was free of the usual arrogance. You smiled and you stole my breath. And there was something in your eyes…a depth, a secret passion that stirred my soul.

There was pain there, too. I know what that feels like. What that looks like. Kindred spirits. Spirits that are weighted down with an old pain that cannot be alleviated.

EVE BLACK

Why am I writing to you? Well, how could I not? I figured that this was much safer than walking up to you and puking all over your work boots. I'm not all that good in social situations, they scare the shit out of me, but I've always been good expressing myself through words. So, here I am, telling you that I love you. Weird, right?

Sorry if you're creeped out by this, that isn't my intention. I am just hoping that this email—despite its unsolicited nature—will bring a smile to your face. Maybe lift your spirits if you're feeling down.

Maybe you'll write back.

Please write back. I promise I'm not a weirdo.

Love, your Secret Admirer,
She Without a Name

chapter TWO

Maeve sat down across from her two newest best friends and tried not to turn tail and run like the hounds of hell were on her heels. They were staring at her, their gazes all too curious. All too seeing.

She could hide from AJ like she was made of air, but Sally and Anna saw *ev-vah-ree-thing*.

"What have you been up to, Mae?" Anna asked, her hazel eyes twinkling. "We haven't seen you in a bit. You been hiding from us?"

Yes! "No, of course not. I'm just busy finishing up all the end of the year admin stuff for the office. You know how those two are—they've left everything to the last minute, and I'm stuck making sure they don't get audited or sued for contract infringement."

Sally sighed, shaking her head, her pin-straight black locks shining beneath the LED lights overhead. "That's my brother, alright." As AJ's sister, Sally knew more about her brother than anyone…except Maeve.

There were things AJ shared in his emails to Swan, She Without a Name, that he never would've shared with his sister. Sex things. As in…his favorite sexual positions, his dirtiest fantasies—bondage—and how and when he lost his virginity. Prom. An affliction he and Maeve shared. But no one could know about how much she knew about AJ. She'd just die.

"And that's definitely Blaze. Those men wouldn't know what the hell to do with themselves if Blaze hadn't poached you from Sylvester to work for Harris," Anna quipped.

"Technically, I still work for Sylvester since he invested in Harris, and Harris is using White tech and resources." Like an email server.

Sally waved off her comment. "Harris pays your wage, so you work for Harris. Sly was sad to see you go from the satellite office, but he understood that you wanted more full-time work."

"He offered me a full-time job with White," Maeve admitted, then immediately regretted it when both Anna and Sally looked at her like she'd grown a second head.

"Why didn't you take it?" Anna asked, planting her elbows on the table to cup her face and stare at Maeve. "I'm sure he could have offered you more money."

It wasn't about the money, it was about getting to spend more time around a man who didn't even know she had tits.

"He offered a salary, which meant I would end up

working odd hours, long hours, and probably weekends. With Harris, I work normal hours and I get my weekends. I sacrifice the income for the chance to actually have a life outside of the office."

Oh, yeah? And what are you doing with all that out-of-office time? Obsessing over her oblivious boss and baking batches of cookies that went straight to her already generous butt.

Sally nodded emphatically. "I get you, girl. I know what you mean. When I worked for Sharp Image Marketing, I worked sixty to eighty hour weeks, and I nearly killed myself. I was hardly home, and when I was, I was usually too exhausted to do anything but change into sweatpants and veg out." Since meeting Sylvester, Sally had definitely undergone a life upgrade. Having a billionaire boyfriend meant she didn't have to work a day in her life, ever again, but the woman was not about to lie down and do nothing. It was against her nature. "I can honestly say that working in consulting for Sly is a much better gig. I get to set my own hours, my own salary, and I get to fuck the boss."

Anna and Maeve chuckled.

"Before all the amazing sex, when she *did* go out, she was a raging bitch," Anna muttered playfully, her eyes dancing.

Sally hit Anna's shoulder, glowering. "I was not! I was my usual charming self, and that paid off with all the hot ass I got on the regular."

From what Maeve knew of Sally's pre-Sylvester dating life, she was a serial one-night stander. It took one night with Sylvester White to change her life forever, however.

And now she's living an HEA most women only read about in romance novels.

"Don't let Sly hear you talking about hot ass that isn't his," Anna chided, grinning.

"And don't let Blaze hear you talking about Sly's hot ass—that man is OTT jealous, possessive of his little Anna-boo."

At Sally's words, Anna's face turned a bright red. Sally cackled and Maeve looked on with jealousy. And self-hatred. She loved her friends, wanted only the best for them, but they also had everything Maeve ever wanted, and it made Maeve feel like shit that she begrudged them their happiness.

Happiness…something you'll never get if you keep up the Swan charade with AJ.

Heaving a sigh, Maeve slipped her hands around her sweating glass of water and leaned back into the red leather booth seat. Did it usually take this long for the waitress to come take their order?

She needed booze—STAT.

Happy Jack's was Anna and Sally's Thursday night hang out spot. It wasn't until a few months ago that they'd invited Maeve to join them. After work, they would meet up, eat bar food, drink a few cocktails, and spill about their weeks. Well, Sally and Anna would spill everything about their weeks, including about their sexy encounters with their men. Maeve talked about work…because spilling the beans about her obsession over Sally's brother would probably get her kicked out of the "sister club".

"So, Mae, take any hotties to bed lately? With an ass like yours, you have to be beating them off with a stick." Anna's eyebrows waggled suggestively.

Maeve huffed, rolling her eyes. "They'd have to know I exist first."

"What do you mean? You're gorgeous—if a little boring in the wardrobe department. I bet, if you put on some skinny jeans, a cute top, and some heels, you'd make every neck in this place snap because they turned to look at you so fast."

"Yeah, if I did that, I'd look like someone stretched too small rubber bands over a bag of pink Playdoh." She snickered humorlessly. "A guy would take one look at me and either run away in horror or vomit." Again, she tried to laugh off her words.

Sally's bright smile fell right off her face, her gaze narrowing. Anger pinched her lovely features until she looked livid enough to light the room on fire.

"Don't you fucking dare talk about yourself like that," she snapped, making Maeve fall back against the booth, her mouth hanging open. "Don't you fucking say shit like that. Do you see me? Anna? Do you think that because we're not size 12s and our thighs touch that we're unfit, unworthy of the love of our men? That we somehow tricked them into loving us and accepting us—hell, *worshipping* us?"

Maeve swallowed, shaking her head. "Of course, not! You two are gorgeous! Sly and Blaze are lucky men," she replied honestly. Sally and Anna were two of the most beautiful and confident women Maeve had ever met. It was one of the reasons Maeve gravitated toward them despite her natural and ingrained awkwardness.

Sally leaned forward as if to lay into Maeve once again, but Anna's gentle hand on Sally's shoulder made the other woman look at her. The tension in her shoulders dipped. Anna braced her elbows against the table, her gaze gliding over Maeve's features, her expression softening.

"I have to tell you something, Mae. I was like you, not that long ago."

"How do you mean?" From what Maeve knew, Anna

and Blaze had been in love with each other for decades. How could Anna possibly know what it felt like to be the gargoyle?

"I know you're probably thinking 'how could Anna be like me? She has the hotness that is Blaze.' Well, I didn't always have Blaze, and there are a few things you need to know. First, Blaze was my best friend for years before we ever became more. For us, it wasn't just about how I never felt like I matched up to the women slinking through his revolving door. It was also about the fact that the asshole honestly believed *he* wasn't good enough for *me*."

"You can't be serious? That man is amazing!" Great boss, honest, loyal, hardworking. He was the ideal man…for someone like Anna. It would only ever be AJ for Maeve.

"Not kidding. Because his father was a sick, sadistic bastard, Blaze grew up believing he couldn't have anything good in his life. He'd been in love with me since high school, but he never acted on it until…well—"

"Anna cut him off like a rotten limb and left his ass flapping in the wind. He realized real quick that he needed to figure his shit out or lose her forever," Sally interjected wryly.

Anna skewered Sally with a glare. "Yeah, that. Second, never base how you feel about yourself on what other people think of you. You will always be your own #1 fan. If you don't like yourself, no one else will, either. Not really. You can't really let anyone else in unless you're accepting of everything that makes up Maeve Thomas."

Oh, that's all it is? It's that easy? she snarked mentally. Nothing was that easy.

The urge to tell them everything about her sorry life slammed into her, building like rushing flood waters behind a dam. Building, pushing. Water rising against the crumbling wall…. Finally, it broke. "It'll never happen, then. I don't know about you, but all my life, all I've ever heard was that I was ugly, fat, useless, worthless, and would never find someone to love me. That's all I ever wanted…someone to love me for me, to see through the layers of fat and weird features to the woman beneath it all."

Anna shook her head and Sally cocked hers to the side, peering into Maeve's eyes. Maeve had expected to see pity or sympathy or surprise on their faces, but she saw none of that. She saw…understanding.

"Whoever made you feel that way should have their teeth punched out, one by one, with the pointy end of a rusty ice skate," Sally declared.

Anna grimaced. "What the hell, Sallina?"

Sally shrugged. "I saw it on *Castaway* with Tom Hanks."

The flood kept coming. "My father. My snobby bitch of a cousin. My step-mother. All the kids in every grade I've ever been in. I didn't even make a real friend until college where I met a pretty cool chick who had far more insecurities than I did…and we just clicked. I admit, I hide behind plain, baggy clothes. I'm trying to keep eyes off my flaws. I'm so sick of the sneers and the looks of disgust, and the comments people don't even bother to whisper. I hide because it's easier than facing down every one."

"But don't you want people to actually *see* you, who you really are?" Anna asked, her brow furrowed.

"Of course, I do. But what are the chances of that happening?"

Sally, the luscious sex goddess she was, clicked her tongue and rolled her eyes, laughing. "You stick with us, we'll get you laid."

Maeve nearly choked on air.

"What? No—"

EVE BLACK

Sally chuckled, her brilliant green eyes, so like her brother's, glimmering mischievously. "What? Don't want to get the love stick in the love tunnel? Don't want to know what it feels like to have a man worship you? There is one out there for you, Maeve, you just have to take a few risks. Now, I know shedding the shit colored skirts is going to be scary, but I honestly think you're beautiful, and if you have a little faith in yourself, you can become the woman you were meant to be."

"I don't know…." Lord, it sounded terrifying, just letting herself peek out from her shell. A shell that even now kept her from the one thing she wanted the most.

AJ Mendez.

Maybe this was what she needed, a little—okay, *big*!— push. Maybe with Sally and Anna's help, she could get her shit together, grow some lady balls, and finally reveal herself to the man she loved.

Can I really do this?

"Come on, Mae," Anna encouraged. "I know Sally can be a bit much, but out of the three of us, she is the curvy sex guru—never a bad body day in her life."

Sally snorted. "That's not true, but I *am* one badass bitch, and I can see you sitting there, crushing on someone, don't think I can't see it in your face." She leaned in, pointing a manicured finger at Maeve's suddenly too warm face. "Whoever he is, give him the best you, the one who is brave and confident, and loves herself—lumps, bumps, and all."

The answer came to her then.

If she wanted AJ, she had to stop letting fear ruin everything. The emails were no longer enough for either of them, and she couldn't spend the rest of her life having a relationship that required internet access. AJ was so patient, so understanding, and so very eager to meet her. He was everything to her…and he deserved the best she could offer him.

Sucking in a deep breath, holding it so long she could feel her lungs burning, and then letting it out in a rush, Maeve strengthened her resolve.

"Okay."

The answering squeals made every head in the bar turn in their direction.

"Fuck yeah!" Sally shouted.

Rather than tuck her head in her chest and pray for invisibility as she usually would in such a situation, Maeve sat up, grinned, and laughed with her friends.

From the Desk of AJ Mendez

December 2nd

Swan...where have you been? I haven't heard from you in a couple of days. I'm worried about you. I got your cookies this morning. Let's just say the courier wasn't all the happy when I practically held him captive to ask him invasive questions about who sent the package. He couldn't give me anything other than it was paid for using a credit card and, of course, he couldn't give me any information on the name on the account.

The cookies are delicious—even better than Lisana made. Is there love in those cookies?

I hope so. I really hope so.

When we finally meet, I'll make you a special dinner. Just the two of us. Candlelight, chilled champagne, and so much fucking love in the food.

My business partner thinks I'm nuts for eating something from someone I never met, but I have met you. My soul has met yours. My match. It is my body that still requires a hands-on introduction. LOL.

Please...respond. If emailing has become a hassle, you can call me. You have my number. I would give anything to hear your voice. Text me, which is quicker and more personal than emailing—in my opinion. I don't care how you reach out, just don't ghost me. Please. Don't disappear on me.

I will take anything from you I can get.
I miss you.

Forever Yours,
AJ

chapter THREE

"I thought we were headed to Happy Jack's to spy on your woman," AJ remarked as he watched his friend flag down a waitress in a bar he hadn't planned to visit that night. When the harried waitress arrived, they ordered two beers—and God, he needed that beer. AJ had been keyed up all day, the need to clock out and head to the beach front dive bar, Happy Jack's, like a Lego in his boot, stabbing at him with every step. There was something about spending time with Anna, Sally, and the competent and quiet office manager, Maeve, that seemed all too important.

Must be missing my sister. Haven't spent enough time with her lately. But what did that have to do with Anna…or

Maeve Thomas? One was his best friend's woman, and the other…. Hmm. He really didn't know what to think about the soft spoken, easily flustered mouse who managed the office like a well-programmed robot.

"I changed my mind. When have you ever had a problem coming to Anchors? Anyway, I figured you and I could use a few brews and some conversation without the girls there to get all up in our business. Well…*your* business, because my lady could get all up in *all* of my business, especially when it comes to my dick."

AJ groaned, rolling his eyes. Ever since Blaze finally pulled his head out of his ass about Anna, they'd been that sweet yet annoying couple people tended to stay away from. All the kissing and caressing in public could really turn the stomach…if he weren't jealous as hell, wanting his own woman to show off and mouth fuck in front of jealous eyes.

"Sly is going to meet us once he's finished some tricky paperwork."

AJ chuckled dryly. "You mean he's actually peeling himself off my sister long enough to spend time with his friends?" At that thought, he pursed his lips, not all that eager to think about his sister and her boyfriend together. And all the things that came with being a couple.

You're just jealous.

Yes and no. No, he wasn't jealous that his sister finally met her one. She deserved to have someone love her and treat her like the queen she was. But, yes, he wanted what they had, that closeness, intimacy, having that one person who belonged to him, and to whom he belonged that he could love. He wanted that someone to go home to, build a home with, and just…have and hold.

Fuck, if any other man heard his thoughts, knew his

heart, they'd call him a pussy, a woman. But he didn't care. All his life he'd yearned for *her*. And he found her...in his Swan.

Slipping his cell from his pocket, he checked the screen.

No new email from Swan. He sighed, his chest constricting. Why hadn't she emailed? It wasn't like her to not send something for so long. Yeah, he'd gotten that box of cookies that morning—they'd been couriered to his house—but he hadn't gotten an email response from her in three days.

Three days too long.

He'd emailed her twice. The first email he sent two days ago was the usual shoot-the-shit, I want to see you in person, I can't get enough of you email. The one he'd sent that afternoon was a little more desperate. He'd thanked her for the cookies...then begged her to email him back. No, he had no fucking shame when it came to his Swan.

There was nothing yet. No response.

Had something happened? Was she injured? Had she finally had enough of his demands and decided he wasn't worth the pestering? No. Not his Swan. She might not be ready to meet in person, but she was just as invested in what they did have as he was. She wouldn't just ghost him...even if there was no clear-cut label for what was going on between them.

Though he wanted to meet her, claim her, and marry the fuck out of her. To him, their label was: meant to be.

Her not responding to his emails was strange. And worrisome.

So...there was something wrong. Right?

He checked his phone again.

"Dude, what the hell? What's so important that you're checking your phone every other minute? Waiting on a call from a hot piece? Now, I might not be single anymore, but I can still be your wingman."

"When have I ever needed a wingman? Besides, all those times we went out before you finally got with Anna, you were the one chasing tail. I was happy with my occasional one-night stand. I wasn't the one who needed to bang random women to try for forget about the woman I really wanted to be with."

Blaze grunted, shame turning his face red. "Yeah, I was a fucking dumbass. No matter how much ass I chased, it just didn't fulfil my need for her."

Of course, it hadn't. Blaze, like AJ's father, had that one woman who loved him, sacrificed for him, sat waiting for him, while he fucked his way through co-eds. Unlike AJ's father, though, Blaze wasn't a sociopathic sadist who enjoyed making his woman live in pain. Blaze was just a careless, stubborn asshole who finally got his shit together.

Unlike Henri Dupree.

"At least you have Anna now, man. Cherish that," AJ urged, his own yearning leaking through and into his words.

Blaze pinned him with a look that told AJ he'd noticed.

"Hmmm...don't think I didn't notice you said 'I *was* happy.'"

"Huh?"

Cocking his lip in a smirk, Blaze explained, "You said, 'I was happy with my occasional one-night stand.' Does that mean you are no longer happy living the bachelor life?"

Hell, no. He was miserable, but he couldn't tell Blaze that. The man was already on his case about his cyber "friendship" with Swan, if he knew that AJ's feelings went deeper than that, Blaze would punch him in the dick so hard his great-grandkids would double over and groan.

Blaze would never understand.

Three months ago, an email from an unknown account hit his inbox. He almost sent it right into the trash bin, but something made him stop. Click. Read. And that had been the beginning of something that had gone from curious questioning to light flirting to downright filthy in a matter of weeks. He assumed from some of the things she wrote that the mystery admirer worked at White and had probably seen him in the Miami office when he'd come into town during those first few months of partnering with Sylvester's company. She'd seen him, fallen for him, and then wrote that first email. And it wasn't just the emails. It was the gifts that came to his office and house. Little things that reminded him of his email conversations with her.

SWAN. She Without a Name.

Boxes of homemade cookies. Cases of his favorite beers. Tickets to Miami Heat games. Books and movies they'd chatted about. Whoever Swan was, she was generous, thoughtful, and damn frustrating. No matter what he promised or how hard he begged, she wouldn't reveal a single detail about herself. And it was driving him fucking crazy!

On paper, she was everything he'd ever wanted: intelligent, witty, funny, flirty, kind, thoughtful, and fucking arousing. But a relationship built on paper was doomed to collapse. For the last month, he'd been pleading with her to meet him in person, to at least send him a picture so he could see her. But she always turned him down, telling him that she wasn't ready for him to see her.

And he'd always wondered why. To him, it didn't matter what she looked like—he'd been into her since that first email, when she admitted that she could see something in him that called to her…because she was the same. Deep down, she was as haunted by old pain as he was. She was his other half. He just had to prove it to her.

"The bachelor life is getting old, man. I'm ready to find my own personal Anna and settle down. I want the house, the white picket fence, the four kids and two dogs. I want it all." And he wanted it with Swan.

Blaze reached across the table and slapped AJ on the shoulder. "You'll get that, man. You deserve it, too, especially after all that shit with your dad."

Blaze, as AJ's best friend, was one of the few who knew the truth about Alejandro Mendez and who he was before he and Sally cut themselves off from their father. Blaze knew about the years of abuse before AJ finally broke away, escaping Savannah to start a new life in Miami. That had been a little over ten years ago. He'd met Blaze while Blaze had been in town doing some shit for the Navy, and they'd hit it off. Once Blaze discharged from the Navy, AJ hooked him up with a job at the construction company where he'd been working since he was eighteen. After a few months, AJ and Blaze decided to move to Blaze's hometown, Jackson Key, and start their own business. The rest was history.

"You guys order food yet?" Sly asked, appearing beside their table, before sliding into the seat across from AJ. He smirked at AJ, knowing full well AJ still felt a little uneasy about the man who was fucking his sister.

The asshole.

"Nah, man. Just drinks. We were shootin' the shit until your ass got here," Blaze answered, raising his hand to flag down the waitress. Apparently, their old waitress clocked out because the new one was….

She appeared in a flash, her bright smile laser focused on him, her interest obvious. Her long blonde hair, big tits, and glittering blue eyes could catch any man's attention. Before Swan, she would have caught his attention. She leaned over AJ, her tits practically spilling from a shirt that could use a few more buttons.

"What can I get you handsome gentlemen?" she purred, sliding a hand over AJ's bicep uninvited. He leaned away. The woman pouted but turned her focus to Sly and Blaze, undeterred. She wanted whichever man gave her the time of day. Ugh.

Blaze coughed, attempting to hide a laugh. "We'll have the eighty hot wings platter with extra ranch dip, the mega nachos with extra guac, and two more pitchers of beer."

Sly kept his focus on the table rather than lift his gaze and give the woman an in. Good. The man was fucking AJ's sister, he'd better keep his eyes to himself.

The waitress, who's nametag—conveniently placed beside the gaping opening in her uniform—read Sandi, gripped AJ's shoulder, rasped that she'd be right back with their drinks in his ear, and then sashayed away, her hips swinging.

Blaze couldn't hold his laughter any longer, barking a guffaw as soon as the woman was out of sight.

"Holy shit, AJ! That woman was about ready to climb into your lap and suck your dick."

AJ rolled his eyes and groaned. "I didn't ask for that." Not that he ever did. Blessed with good looks, a built body he earned from working hard, and an easy smile, most women just fell into his lap—sometimes literally. At first, it had been fun as hell, getting ass whenever he wanted it without the work most men had to put in. He reveled in it. Once his mom died, however, the fun leached from that lifestyle. Yeah, he still got ass whenever he wanted it, but he fucked with moderation. In his twenty-nine years, he'd never had an actual relationship with a woman, just empty sexual encounters that satiated his need for sex, but left him feeling cold.

Now, he was over meaningless sex. He wanted that relationship, that intimacy, that closeness with one person who filled his heart and soul with contentment.

Swan.

Fuck. He really needed to focus on something else, otherwise Blaze would figure it out and climb up his ass about it.

Sly laid his phone on the table and smirked at AJ. "Your sister, Anna, and Maeve are hitting Velvet Saturday night."

Velvet was the new nightclub in Tampa that his sister had been harping on about for weeks. Apparently, she'd finally worn Sly down enough to get him to let her go. Not that his sister ever required permission to do whatever the fuck she wanted, but she loved her boyfriend enough to give him the *illusion* of being in charge.

Blaze grumbled. "Guess I am, too."

AJ grinned, picturing a grumpy as hell Blaze tossing metrosexual males off the dance floor. His smile slipped when the image in his head switched from a bitching Anna to a cowering Maeve.

Maeve Thomas, in a dance club, actually dancing and not hiding in the corner? Nah, that wouldn't happen. That woman spent more time hiding in plain sight than any woman he'd ever met. He knew she thought no one noticed her unless they wanted something from her, but that was the furthest thing from the truth. He noticed her…he just didn't think she'd appreciate why.

Maeve was a mouse. Dressed in shades of brown a gray, speaking in a soft, unobtrusive voice, sort of scurrying out of the way whenever AJ entered the office. He couldn't understand what it was about him that made her so anxious.

And that "not knowing" made her all the more intriguing—which he would never admit to anyone.

The Harris Construction LLC office manager was a curious creature, and it annoyed him that he was curious in the first place. She was an employee, one of his sister's friends, and generally a beige personality. So why was the thought of her in the club bothering him?

"Guess we're all going to Velvet on Saturday night," AJ interjected, making Blaze's eyebrows shoot up in surprise.

AJ grabbed his cell to check for a new email, willfully ignoring the knowing smile on his friend's face.

chapter
FOUR

SALLY SLAPPED MAEVE'S HAND, MAKING HER YELP. Maeve had been tugging on the hem of the shockingly red bandage wrap dress Sally had demanded Maeve buy and wear for their evening at the club.

When Maeve had blabbered about the dress being too expensive to wear only once, both Sally and Anna took turns trying to convince Maeve that the dress was an investment in her future.

A future of public shaming and humiliation, maybe.

Finally, Sally had commented about how Maeve would never land her "mystery" crush if she kept hiding behind brown bags.

EVE BLACK

The dress hugged every lump and crevice, like a sheet of plastic wrap. The bottom of the dress hit just beneath her ass, and the top of the dress covered her nipples and not much else. Thankfully, the dress had wide enough straps to hide the balconette bra she had to wear to keep her boobs off the dance floor. With a 48D rack, Maeve was used to hiding her tatas behind bulky, flouncy blouses. The bandage dress hid *nuh-thing*. She felt like everyone was going to take one look at her and cover their eyes in horror.

When Sally was done fussing with Maeve's hair and makeup, there'd been a minute there when Maeve had actually felt sexy. The reflection that peered back at her was one that both shocked and excited her. Her body was big but the dress didn't look half bad, and the hair and makeup made her look like a model on a magazine cover.

The heels Sally gave her—glittering gold with bright red bottoms—made her legs look long and toned. Being only five-foot-six, the heels performed a miracle.

A miracle she hoped proved truly miraculous.

Anna and Sally were adamant that Maeve would catch some eyes that night, and Maeve wanted to believe them, especially since she wanted to make getting all dressed up worth the hassle. But…Maeve really wanted a *specific* someone to notice her. Too bad he wasn't going to be at the club that night.

Maeve tugged on the hem again, nervously wishing the fabric at least met the middle of her thigh. When she stood up, her ass would practically be hanging out, which only made Sally all the more determined to get Maeve into a pair of thong panties.

Earlier that evening, when she was dressing, she'd thought, 'what the hell, might as well go all out if I'm going

Adoring **ALEJANDRO**

to die of embarrassment.' Now, though, as they were pulling up to the club, she was rethinking all of her adult life choices.

"Stop! If you keep pulling on it, you'll rip it, and I won't let you go home and change. You'll have to spend the night flashing your panties at everyone," Sally pronounced from the far passenger door of the hired car Sly had ordered for them for the evening.

Sally knew better than to think her boyfriend would just let her go out without supervision, but he at least let her arrive at the club without him breathing down her back about her outrageously tight and revealing wrap dress that emphasized more than it covered. She was all curves, ass, and sass, and not for the first time, Maeve wished she was as confident in her body as Sally was.

The driver opened the door on Maeve's side and offered a hand. Sucking in a breath, she slid from the car, determined to ignore the urge to pull her dress down.

She stood on the sidewalk outside the club and stared.

The line was longer than the block, wrapping around the large building and disappearing. If she had to wait in that line and then spend the night standing and dancing, she'd lose all feeling in her toes from the pretty but pinchy heels.

Velvet was a trendy Florida nightclub. The club was housed within an old industrial factory building that had been renovated from gritty to glitzy—at least that's what the write up in the newspaper said. From what Maeve could see, it looked just the right amount of sexy and fun.

"Come on," Sally effused, linking her arm with Maeve's and then Anna's arms, and dragging them straight to the menacing looking bouncer at the door.

"Sly and Sallina," Sally drawled haughtily, as though those two words were enough to—

"You're in," the large, bald man grumbled, stepping away from the door to allow them entrance.

Her mouth hanging open, Maeve didn't even have time to blink before she was stepping from the crisp fall evening and into a wickedly sensual heat wave.

Dark with red and gold lights shining in predetermined areas, the large room was perfectly shadowed along the booths, bar, and dance floor to allow people to either laugh in the light or moan in the dark.

"Forget the drinks for now, let's dance before the guys get here and turn into the fun police."

That was the first Maeve heard that Sly and Blaze were coming. She should have figured that they would, though. Those two men were outstandingly possessive of their women.

And Lord, she was jealous of that.

It was on the tip of her tongue to ask if AJ was coming, too, but she stopped herself just in time. It wouldn't do to tip Sally off that the crush of Maeve's was the unattainable AJ Mendez, her older brother.

Tugging her behind them, Sally maneuvered through the crowd with Maeve practically tripping over her feet to remain upright. Before she knew what the hell was happening, she was surrounded by bodies, all gyrating to a Harry Styles song with an EDM twist.

Who thought "Watermelon Sugar" could be a pulsating dance song?

"Come on, lady, I know you have some moves," Anna yelled into Maeve's ear to be heard over the volume of the music and people.

The first strains of "For the Now" by Kovich featuring

adoring **ALEJANDRO**

Annie Bosko began pumping through the speakers, and Maeve couldn't stop the smile that spread over her face.

Dragging Anna closer, she yelled, "I love this song!" Anna grinned, her sweaty, flushed face lovelier than ever.

Maeve had first heard the on an episode of *Driven* a sexy TV show streaming on Passionflix, and she'd added it to Spotify playlist to listen to whenever she needed a pick-me-up.

Let loose! Enjoy the moment. Live for the now.

For a moment, she'd forget that she was an unloved child. A fat mess of a woman. A shadow of what she should be. For a moment, she was someone else. Someone worthy of the male eyes staring at her with dark lust. For a moment, she was alive.

Stop hiding.
Stop.
Hiding.

The pulse of the music, pounding, thrumming, vibrating, moved through her. Lighting her nerve endings on fire, scorching her blood, liquefying her bones.

Taking over.

Her hips moving, her smile growing wider, she threw her arms into the air and let the music take her away.

AJ couldn't believe his eyes. Had he somehow tripped and entered another dimension? Because there was no way that the sexy as hell vixen dressed in red, dancing between two grabby assholes was his mousy, unassuming office manager.

Shit!

Seriously, who was this woman? Because it couldn't be

the same woman who hid behind her computer screen, boxy clothes, and quiet manner.

Usually, he'd ignore her obvious discomfort and just get his work done. It wasn't his business that she preferred to be as inconspicuous as possible even in a working office environment. It did bother him, though, that perhaps she felt unwelcome at Harris Construction. He'd even brought it up with Blaze and Sly, but they'd assured him that she was just shy. He'd shrugged it off and tried not think about it again.

She was just his employee. There was where it began and ended.

So what was with that comment about cookies the other day, you degenerate?!

That had been a mistake, something he wouldn't repeat. Honestly, he had no idea what had come over him in that moment other than the immediate need to see the straight-laced, buttoned-up mouse blush.

And boy had she.

Tonight, though, the idea of her blushing on top of everything else about her….

A tightening began in his chest…and his jeans.

Tight as fuck red dress that barely covered her luscious ass, thick legs that went on forever and would feel amazing curved around his waist. Big, plump breasts that were spilling over the top of her dress with just a peek-a-boo of a black lace bra—enough that they would overflow his hands as he cupped them lovingly. Hair that was usually tied back into a bun was in loose, glossy golden hair down to the middle of her back, and would work perfectly as a tether to hold her head in place while he kissed the shit out of her. And the smile on her face, bright, coy, and so joyous, it changed everything he ever thought of mousy Maeve Thomas.

adoring ALEJANDRO

She was fucking gorgeous. The body of a goddess sent to earth to ensnare him and claim his soul.

And she was surrounded by barracudas eager to sink their teeth into her soft looking flesh.

"What are you staring at with that look on your face?" Sly asked, pushing up beside him to follow his line of sight. "Maeve?" AJ couldn't mistake the sound of surprise in Sly's voice.

Of course, it's a surprise. The man had known Maeve for months longer than AJ, having worked for White in Miami before coming to Jackson Key, and AJ had never shown even an inkling of interest in the woman.

Interest? There's no interest. She's an employee…and perhaps a friend. That's all. He was worried about her, that was all. Unlike Sally, who thrived on male attention, Maeve was out of her element. Right?

She doesn't look like it, his inner voice growled.

No. She didn't. She looked…breathtaking. Sensual. Like that dress had been painted on with loving hands…hands that should have been his.

Wait. *What the fuck?!*

"I'm just surprised to see her like that," AJ answered honestly, though there was far more to it than that. He was knocked off kilter. His head spinning. His world tipping. His notions about one woman exploding in the water. "She's going to get herself in trouble."

Sly chuckled, slapping AJ on the back. "Looks like she doesn't mind." He pointed to the enamored throng closing in on Maeve. A cluster of men staring openly, checking her out, and a few men moving in close enough to rub themselves against her.

"Sally and Anna should be with her," AJ snapped,

wondering where the hell his sister was and what the hell she was thinking bringing Maeve to the club—and dressed like that.

"They're right there," Sly answered, tipping his chin toward where Sally and Anna were dancing with each other not more than a few feet away, their gazes locked on their friend, their faces bright with wicked grins.

They *wanted* Maeve to get fucking mauled!

Without giving himself a moment to actually think about what the hell he was doing, he pushed away from the wall where he'd been standing, sipping a beer, and headed toward the center of the throng of admirers.

Shoving assholes out of the way, he was soon standing before a flushed, smiling Maeve, his heart racing.

Startled, Maeve looked up at him, her brilliant smile falling from her face. The loss of it like a steel pike through his chest. Why couldn't she smile at him like she had at those other men?

Because you're her boss, and you're coming to ruin her fun.

Fuck that! That woman was headed for a catastrophic mistake if she continued to invite every leering jackass in the club to come touch her.

They had no right to touch her, to even stand as close as they were. He refused to listen to the sneering voice in his head grumbling that the right was his alone. Because that was bullshit. She wasn't *his*, either.

"AJ?" Maeve breathed, pushing strands of hair off her face where they'd stuck to her forehead. She was sweaty, her cheeks pink, her eyes bright and shiny, like two precious sapphires in flames.

Beautiful.

Shaking himself, he grabbed her shoulder and glowered down at her.

"What the hell do you think you're doing?" he barked, making Maeve jerk, her once straight shoulders and loose frame drooping and tensing.

Shit, fuck! He didn't mean for her to crawl back into her shell. He only meant for her to…. *To what? She was having a good time and you ruined it.*

But those men were too close. Touching her.

Like you want to.

Fuck, shit!

Sally and Anna pushed in beside Maeve and glared at him. Sally slapped his hand where it was gripping Maeve a little too tightly. "What the hell are you doing? She was just dancing, enjoying herself. You're the one barging in like an asshole," Sally spat.

Behind him, Sly and Blaze muttering something to one another under their breath, which only made AJ all the more pissed.

He *was* acting like an asshole, which was so out of character for him, but he just couldn't stop himself. He'd seen Maeve, saw the other men, and the need to protect had hit him so hard, it felt like his ribs were cracking under the force.

AJ couldn't give an answer that didn't make him look like a jerk, so he kept his mouth shut and took a step back.

Maeve's expression was closed, her once bright eyes dimmed.

Goddammit!

"Come on, Mae, let's grab some drinks. Maybe AJ will have chilled the hell out by then," Anna said, glaring at AJ before pulling Maeve into her arms and leading her through the crowd and toward the bar.

Tension rolled through him, his body thrumming—and not from the Night Panda song blasting through the crowded, humid room.

What the hell had possessed him to do that? That wasn't him.

No. It was *her*. Something about *her* had driven him to momentary madness.

"Well, that was a clusterfuck, man." Blaze handed AJ a cold beer, which he downed in four gulps.

Sly handed AJ a heavy truth. "I think she got under your skin."

No fuck, he mentally snarked.

And it didn't slip his notice that he hadn't thought of Swan all night.

chapter
FIVE

THE WEEKEND HAD BEEN LONG AND TORTUROUS. After the embarrassing hell that was Saturday night, Maeve had spent all of Sunday nursing her wounded pride. And a gallon of mint chocolate chip ice cream. And a 6-pack of hard apple cider. And hours of *Supernatural*. She gorged herself on Dean Winchester and carbs. And she felt like shit.

For a foolish moment Saturday night, she'd shucked her shell, owned her curves, and believed she was attractive as Sally and Anna had said. That the men who introduced themselves to her were interested in her and wanted to dance with her. That her fears and insecurities were unfounded. That she could actually be a woman men wanted.

But one look at AJ's disgusted, angry face, and she'd been clobbered with the truth. She'd been fooling herself. She was just a fat, ugly idiot—like she'd always been.

Her hope that AJ would want to be with *her* once she revealed herself as Swan had been dashed.

Now, she had to face the man at work.

Monday morning was hell on earth, like it was every Monday morning, really, but this Monday morning was especially hellish. She'd arrived at work early in order to get behind the door of her office before AJ got there. Usually, Mondays were admin days for AJ and Blaze, so they were in their offices, doing paperwork until clocking out at five. Once in a while, they'd knock on her door to ask her a question or give her some documents. Today, though, she had a feeling AJ would avoid her like the plague.

Diving into work, Maeve ignored the aches and pains of sitting in one spot for too long, and kept at it. She'd take a break once her bladder got too full to ignore and she had to pee. Until then, she'd remain where she was, doing her job, and ignoring the man she loved but could never have.

A heavy knock sounded on the door, making her jump. Her heart racing, she blinked and looked at the time. It was 4:51 P.M. The day had gone by much faster than she'd expected. Fortunately, when she'd taken a potty and lunch break earlier, AJ was nowhere to be seen. Yup. Avoiding her.

So, who was knocking on her door?

"Yeah?" she called, her voice squeaking. *No wonder he thinks of you as a mouse*—a phrase she'd overheard him calling her once or twice.

"Maeve...can we talk?"

AJ.

Dammit!

No! she wanted to scream, but how pointless was that? The man was there, once again blocking her only escape route. He probably wanted to talk about what happened Saturday night, which would only make her feel worse.

Get it over with, then you can go home, eat more ice cream, and watch more Sam and Dean.

Sighing, she said, "Come in." *Go away!*

There was a small hesitation. She held her breath, wondering if he'd changed his mind, then the latch swiveled down and the door slowly swung open.

AJ stuck his head through the crack, a forced smile on his face. How did she know it was forced? Because she knew every smile, every frown, every expression, and every word of his body language. She'd studied him from afar—and sometimes up close—long enough and with enough diligence to be an expert.

Right now, the man was uncomfortable and uncertain. *Good, at least it isn't just me.*

"Hey," he began, slipping his whole body into her office and shutting the door behind him without taking his gaze off of her. "I know it's the end of the day, but I was wondering if I could speak with you for a moment."

So formal. Like a boss.

He is *your boss. Period. So what if you know every single one of his kinky sex fantasies. Like tying you up and licking your body inch by inch, or painting your breasts and pussy in warm chocolate and feasting on you?* She'd made herself come to those fantasies more than once since she'd read that email. But he hadn't meant for her to know those things, had he?

He didn't know he was sharing that with you, and once he finds out....

God, she had no idea what to expect. Sexual harassment suit? Unemployment? A public shunning?

Him dragging you into the closest room, shoving you against the door, and fucking you, which is also one of his fantasies?

Yeah, like that would happen.

She hadn't said anything, as lost as she was in her own thoughts, so AJ continued, his anxiousness showing in his hands which were cupping the back of his neck and rubbing at the stubble on his square jaw.

Two nervous gestures at once. Score.

Ugh. He looked so tasty. Why did he have to look like a snack?

"It's about Saturday night...at Velvet," he explained, making her stomach drop into her black ballet flats.

"I didn't mean to make you feel bad, Maeve, I really didn't. My intention wasn't to ruin your night."

"Then why? Why did you do it?"

Silence filled her small office as his expression shuddered. He crossed her arms and drew in a deep breath.

"You're friends with my sister and Anna...and I'd like to consider myself your friend as well."

"So, you were acting as my *friend* when you hurt me?" She couldn't believe this was happening. Friends. Friend-zoned.

"Dammit, this is coming out all wrong," he grumbled, his beautiful face pinching, his jaw clenching in aggravation. Why did he have to be sexy even when he was being an ass?

"What I mean is that...well, like Sally, I think of you as a brother would a sister. An overprotective brother who wants to keep his sister safe from men who would use them, hurt them, and then throw them away."

Now, he thinks of me as a sister? Sister was worse than being friend-zoned. At least as friends, there was a slight chance of there being more. As his sister, it would be impossible. Heart shattered. She should have known.

No man could ever look at her and picture more with her.

But he pictures more with Swan. Yeah, but she wasn't real. *She is. She is you when you aren't hiding behind your weight and fear.*

Standing from her desk, she marched toward him.

"Do you usually look at your sister with disgust on your face?" Angry, frustrated, Maeve couldn't filter her words. "Do you usually make your sister feel like she was making a fool of herself?"

His eyes wide, his naturally tanned face paled. AJ threw his hands up, waving them frantically. "What? No! That isn't what I meant. I'm not disgusted by you, Maeve. Far from it. I—"

He cut himself off, his mouth slamming shut.

Deep within her, hope once more sparked to life. He wasn't disgusted by her. Far from it. What was he going to say that made him clam up like that?

"What do you mean, AJ? If I don't disgust you, what could you possibly have to say that will make this all better? Because from where I was standing on Saturday night, you thought I was too fat and ugly to be shaking my ass and begging those men for attention."

His eyes narrowing, their emerald depths turning to green fire, he growled, "That's bullshit, and you know it! You're fucking gorgeous, Maeve. A total goddamn knock out. And I was pissed that all those men were too close, and you were too naïve to realize the danger you were in."

Her mouth dropped open as she gasped.

Her voice came out thready, breathy, like she'd just run a mile. "You think I'm gorgeous?" she asked…then the rest of his words clattered through her hazy brain. "Wait…you think I'm naïve?"

"Not naïve as much as…reckless. In the office, you're this quiet, unassuming…mouse. It's like you hide and hope no one notices you. Then, at Velvet, you were…someone else. And I couldn't believe that you could possibly know what you were getting yourself into. Sally and Anna pushed you too far—"

Mouse.

Mousy Maeve.

Brown and boring and small and quiet.

And forgettable.

Hurt turned to vitriol in her blood, rising into her chest to burn right through her fear. Maeve growled, her eyes narrowing on the asshole standing before her. "Watch it! Those women did nothing but pull me out of my shell and help me feel amazing. At first, yeah, I was uncomfortable. That dress wasn't my first or hundredth choice of attire. But once we got there, and I started having a good time, I actually felt good about myself for the first time in a long time." She watched his expression harden, his nostrils flaring. His green eyes darkening. Maeve stepped toward him once more, raising a single finger, and poking him in his hard chest. "Then you came and ruined everything. Why would you do that?" *Poke.* "What right did you have to step in where you weren't wanted? Despite whatever fucked up idea you have in your head, I am not your goddamn sister. And, right now, I don't even want to be your friend." *Poke.*

He grabbed her finger, holding it captive against his chest where his heart was racing. Her breath caught—his eyes peered down at her, dark and devastating.

"You don't want to be my friend, Maeve? Well that's too fucking bad, because you can't be anything else, despite how goddamn sexy you are. Despite how much I wanted to rip off that fucking red dress and devour you. Despite how many times I've fucked my own hand, thinking about those curves of yours wrapped around me, beneath me."

Maeve couldn't think, couldn't speak. She could only breathe, her chest heaving with the increase in blood flow as lust flooded through her body.

"Y-you don't mean that," she rasped, the words escaping in short gasps.

AJ stepped closer, his height making her look up. She blinked, unable to fathom what the hell was happening. She was in her office with AJ…and something was happening between them.

Could this be it? That moment when he realized they were meant to be together?

He crowded her, his rock-hard body brushing against her sensitive breasts, her nipples pert and aching. Something else rock hard pressed against her belly. Long. And. Hard. Pressing against the soft rolling flesh of her stomach.

Good Lord, the man was huge.

AJ cupped her face, the roughness of his work worn hands like fine grit sandpaper, gently sliding over sensitized skin. She shuddered at the sensation, her body trembling at his touch.

Finally.

He leaned in, the scent of spice, sweat, and hardworking male filled her nostrils, making her dizzy with the need to lick if off him. He was close, his mouth a mere inch from hers. His hot breaths fluttered over her face, tickling her eyelids and cheeks. He sucked in a deep breath, closed his eyes, and groaned.

He eyes popped open. Dark. Hungry. His gaze dropped to her lips.

"Fuck. I need to taste you," he growled, before slamming his mouth to hers.

His large, callused hands, holding her head in place, her devoured her.

Hot. Devastating. Shattering. Ravenous. With each lap of his tongue, he ravaged her, pouring in emotion—desire, need, possessiveness, aggression. There was nothing she could do but give, and give, as he took. Stealing her thoughts, robbing her of breath and strength. She collapsed against him, her sensitive breasts with pebbled nipples rubbing against the hard expanse of his chest. Never in her life had she known such scorching lust.

His tongue sparred with hers, forcing her compliance, and she moaned into his mouth, even as he groaned into hers.

Yes. Take.

Her heart hammering, Maeve raised her arms, ready to thread her fingers behind his head, but he jerked as if coming awake, breaking their kiss, and shoving her backward.

"Fuck!" He palmed his face, rubbing at it like he was trying to wash her off. Wash off what they'd done. "Fuck! That wasn't supposed to happen. That *cannot* happen." He dropped his hands and cursed again, finally meeting her gaze.

Shame. Regret. Guilt. It was all plain as day, written

into the furrows in his brow, the stress creases around his mouth and eyes, and the way his eyes were dark and hollow.

Humiliation rose up to suffocate her. She stumbled back, her ass hitting her desk and holding her upright when her legs gave out.

"I'm sorry, Maeve. I didn't mean for this to happen. Forgive me."

She dragged in a breath. "What's wrong with it? We're two adults…and I wanted that kiss." She marveled at the bravery it took to admit that. She drew in another breath and steeled her spine. She could do this. "And I know you wanted it, too. You wouldn't have done it otherwise."

He shook his head, closing his eyes. The lips she'd kissed thinned.

"Yes, I wanted to kiss you, you're an attractive woman, Maeve. But I can't do this—whatever this is. I…I'm involved with someone else."

That shook her…and not because it hurt, but because she knew who that someone else was.

Swan.

Her.

"Oh?" she asked, forcing a tone of disappointment.

He sighed, his expression softening. "Again, I'm sorry, Maeve. I just…I want to be with someone else. No hard feelings, right? We can be friends, right?"

"Right." *Fuck that!*

He nodded, offering her a slight smile, one that didn't reach his eyes.

The door was open and AJ's back disappeared through it, just as a small victorious smile touched her lips.

That kiss changed everything.

From the Desk of SWAN

October 1st

Wow. You actually wrote me back. I'm happy yet shocked. I was worried that you'd think I was some sort of freak or fraud.

Thank you.

So....you want to know more about me, eh? Well, I'm a woman in my mid-twenties. I have a job I enjoy. I live in a beautiful town. I have a coffee mug collection that is out of control. And I think you are the most beautiful man I have ever seen. Yup, I said it. It's surprising how honest one can be when hiding behind a computer screen. And I guess that's what all those romance novels are about. Not that I read those. Much.

But that isn't what this is. This is all too real. This is about a woman who fell for a man who doesn't know she exists. You guessed it—we've met before. But you won't remember me. For me, though…. When I first saw you, my heart stopped. I literally stopped breathing for long seconds. I couldn't take my eyes off you. Tall, tanned, dark-haired, with those gorgeous green eyes that just draw you in, strip you naked, and make you beg. God…and your body. Hard. So hard. Perfectly hewn from hard work and not the gym like some dude-bro. If I could dream up the perfect man for me, you would appear.

Lord, I know I sound crazy, but I felt so drawn to you, I just had to email you. To let you know how I feel even though nothing can come of it. I'll just have to be content with this…if you continue replying, that is.

Hoping you reply,

Yours,
SWAN

chapter SIX

HIS MUSCLES ACHED, BUT IT WAS A GOOD ACHE. IT WAS the kind of ache that came with a full day of hard labor. His two hands, his back, his legs, his strength helped built four walls of a small cottage where a family, someday soon, would spend their summer vacation. They'd pull up their jammed-packed family van, spill out with wide eyes and road trip cramps, and they'd see their vacation home for the first time. A beach house where they will create family memories that will last them a lifetime.

Good memories.

Happy memories.

Memories that would make them smile years from now,

when their lives got difficult and they needed that sliver of joy to push them through it.

Those are the types of memories he was building with Harris Construction. They were building houses, yes, but AJ knew they were doing more than that.

He was gifting families with opportunities he never had.

Henri Dupree on a family vacation with his wife and kids? Fuck that. The man spent enough time gallivanting across the Mediterranean with French models, Brazilian songstresses, and even the occasional waitress…or five. He was too busy getting his dick wet on his own to ever take his family on a vacation.

Not that AJ gave a damn about that. But he had wished for more for his sister. For his mother, who left him a sizable inheritance when she died. Not to mention the billionaire paternal grandfather who loved to spoil his only two grandchildren with monthly allowances they couldn't even begin to spend. No one knew that AJ and Sally were wealthy. They both abjectly hated that their well spring was paid for by their mother's misery and suicide. And their grandfather's money, while not tainted, was still shadowed by the last name Dupree. So, rather than use that money to fund a lifestyle he despised, he was paying it forward through funding charities for lower class families who couldn't afford the costs of a family vacation. Some of those funds went into building cottages like the one he built that day. Some of the funds went to a balloon account that the family could use for trip expenses like fuel, food, and activities.

Since creating the charity, Building Memories, AJ and Harris Construction, LLC. had built or remodeled fifteen small beach cottages in Jackson Key, Tampa, Miami, Clearwater, and New Port Richey. In total, Building

Memories had funded the lifelong memories of more than two hundred families.

Damn, it felt good to have a purpose. One that helped to clear the muck and miasma that came with his DNA.

By blood, he was a Dupree, something he couldn't scrub from his body no matter how many times he made himself bleed with the effort. By purpose and deed, he was a Mendez. Something he was proud of.

Ugh. Too deep for the end of a long day.

At least he wasn't thinking about that kiss. Or the woman who'd made him harder than he'd ever been in his life. Her soft moans of pleasure had hit him right in the dick, driving him mad with the need to strip her bare right in her office, and feed his throbbing cock into her wet pussy.

Dammit! Now he couldn't stop thinking about her. And he shouldn't be. But no matter how many times he told himself she was off-limits, his employee, and that he was dedicated to Swan—even if they'd never actually met—he couldn't shake the feeling that Maeve Thomas was someone special.

It just wouldn't be to him. It couldn't be.

Sighing, AJ started his truck, eager to get home, soak his muscles in a hot shower, and have a cold beer or two. Nearing seven o'clock, the streets of Jackson Key were just starting to empty out of work day traffic. The cars moving down the main drag were headed out for dinner, drinks, or heading home from the beach.

Turning onto Station Street, headed toward his condo, something on the opposite side of the road caught his attention.

A silver sedan with rusty wheel wells, one of which was missing a tire.

adoring ALEJANDRO

Beside the crippled car was the one woman he'd been trying to avoid all day.

Maeve was staring down at a tire on its side on the road. Her hands were planted on her ample hips, which were being hugged by a skirt that caressed her hips and thighs, and cupped her ass just right.

Fuck!

Where had all her formless beige clothes go?

Slowing to pull up behind her, AJ cursed his luck. He couldn't just leave her there; she needed help, and he was more than capable of changing a tire.

Jumping from his truck, he strode to her. She hadn't noticed him yet, her attention pinned to the empty wheel well. He could see wisps of her blonde hair clinging to her forehead and cheeks. It been sweltering that day, which was somewhat strange for Florida in the fall, and Maeve was wearing clothing more suitable to an air-conditioned office than to the side of a road. Her long-sleeved teal blouse cupped her large tits, but fluttered loosely around her belly. He couldn't imagine how warm was she wearing the long skirt and the blouse, but it couldn't be comfortable.

So, invite her to remove it all, piece by piece, until she's naked, bared to you so you can look your fill.

No! *Get your fucking head on straight!* "Hey, what happened?"

Squeaking, her hand flying to her chest, and said chest heaving, Maeve spun toward him, her ocean eyes large and frightful. Damn, she really had been lost in her thoughts.

Her total focus on him now, she dropped her hand from her chest, though his gaze stayed there a few moments longer before jerking up to meet hers.

"What were you thinking about so hard that you didn't hear my Hemi diesel truck pull up behind you?"

Her full cheeks pinkened, her expression filling with guilt.

And now he *really* wanted to know what she was thinking about so hard.

"Oh. AJ." She laughed nervously. "Well…my tire came off, so I was thinking about how I was going to get it back on, and if I couldn't do that, how I was going to see about a tow, and then how I was going to get home, and then how I was going to get to work tomorrow…." Her words trailed off as her cheeks grew even more pink. "I'm sorry. I ramble when I get nervous."

He opened his mouth to ask her what she was so nervous about, wanting to know if the memory of their kiss in her office was messing with her as much as it was messing with him, instead he asked something less provocative.

"The tire came off while you were driving the car?"

"Um. Yeah. I was driving and then the car started to shake, and then the back of the car started to fish tail, and then there was this loud thudding noise. By the time I stopped, the tire was just hanging off. I had no idea what I was doing, so I grabbed the car jack and pull the wheel the rest of the way off."

Moving closer to her, he couldn't stop the instinctual inclination to take a deep breath…and fill his lungs with her scent.

Vanilla…and something fruity. His mouth watered.

Get a grip! Squatting, he scanned the tire, immediately finding the issue.

"This tire is fucking bald, Maeve. I'm surprised it didn't blow and send you into oncoming traffic."

adoring **ALEJANDRO**

She huffed, crossing her arms over her chest, which only made AJ's eyes land there as well. The tops of her breasts pushed up, cresting the top of her blouse, peeking over at him as if to tease him with the promise of soft, sweet flesh. His hands twitched to cup them, to squeeze them, to claim them as his.

His cock thickened in his jeans. Shooting to his feet, he turned away from Maeve, moving around to the other side of the car to inspect the other tires…and hide his hard on from her.

"I meant to buy a new one and get it put on, but I…well…I got distracted last weekend and I forgot."

"Oh? What were you doing that was so important you nearly caused a car accident?"

She glared at him over the top of her dated car. The paint on the roof was chipped and peeling, revealing patches of rust there, too. He just stopped himself from asking how old the damn thing was, and then demanding she tow the junk heap to the scrap yard.

His dick now under control, he walked back to the other side of the car to stand beside her, drawn to be near her. Wanting to pull her into his arms, run his nose along her neck, and then feast on her lips once more.

"Don't take the tone with me. I'm not an idiot," she snapped. "And I was baking."

His eyebrows touched his hairline. "*Baking* was the distraction that kept you from getting a new tire?"

"Yep," she replied, popping the "P". She dropped her gaze from his to lean into her car. He didn't even bother stopping his gaze from landing on her lush ass. Two perfectly round, bouncing globes. They'd be pale, smooth. Soft. And they'd jiggle like crazy as he pounded into her from behind, his eyes watching his fat cock disappear into her stretched pussy.

With his mind on fucking her, he was too preoccupied to listen to her conversation with the tow company. When she finished the call, he snapped out of his haze, picking up the bald tire and throwing it into the back of his truck.

"I'll toss that," he said. "How long did they say?"

"Twenty minutes, but he said to leave the keys in the car if I wanted to go." The look she gave him, told him she was. She was sweaty, looked exhausted, and he wanted to take care of her. The urge to reach out and peel the damp hair from her cheek was near overwhelming. He shoved his hands into his pockets instead.

"I can take you home. I'd pick you up in the morning, but I have to be at the Powell site at six."

She smiled, waving him off. "That's fine. I'll just take an Uber in the morning. The guy, Jerry, said he'd take the car to his garage, so I'll have to Uber there tomorrow afternoon, but none of that is your problem. I'm just grateful you stopped. If I had to stand here in the heat, feeling out of my depth, I think I would have screamed." She sniffed an adorable laugh.

He smiled, winking. "Glad to be your white knight, milady."

Giggling, she followed him to his truck, climbing in when he opened the passenger door. He watched her. Didn't touch her. Even though her perfect ass had been right in his face. He wanted to bite it, to see if it was firm enough to take the pressure, or if it would give as he pressed his teeth into her creamy flesh.

Fuck! When did he become a biting fetishist? Damn, he really needed to get a grip. Then get laid. And not with Maeve.

adoring ALEJANDRO

Swan. He needed to get Swan to meet him so he could be with her. Months and months' worth of pent-up sexual need was turning him into something he didn't recognize. In his twelve years of sexual history, he'd never gone two weeks without sex, let alone almost four months. It was obviously rotting his brain.

Back in his truck, Maeve gave him direction to her apartment, which wasn't all that far from his condo. He pulled up outside in under five minutes, turning off the ignition and turning toward her. He meant to say goodbye and tell her he'd see her tomorrow in the office, but the words wouldn't come.

In the dwindling light of the setting sun, the glow of fire streaming into the truck's cabin struck Maeve, creating a halo around her that stole his breath. Her heat flushed face shone, her eyes twinkling. Her lips, spread into a smile, were pink, plump, kissable.

His body tensed, the need to drag her into him and take her mouth made his breath catch. When had this woman become his weakness? No longer the mouse he could ignore, she'd transformed into a siren, calling to him, seducing him without even touching him.

He needed to get out of there. Drop her off, leave, and the spend the next however long it took to get the lust from his system, trying to avoid her.

Maeve tucked a strand of golden hair behind her ear, ducking her face shyly. "Uh…come in? I mean, the least I can do is offer you something to drink."

Don't do it! "Sure."

chapter SEVEN

Her second-floor apartment was small but homey. Warm colors, pictures hung on the walls, soft, comfortable looking furniture, and not too much clutter. It looked lived in and loved.

The air conditioning kicked on, sending a blast of cold air into the room. Skin moist with perspiration prickled, sending tingles through his body. Goosebumps rose on his arms.

A quick glance at Maeve's chest told him the temperature change affected her too; her nipples pert and hard beneath her blouse.

As she headed off to change, AJ stood in her kitchen,

taking in the small but immaculate space. Every appliance was in its place, and the counters were clean. The only thing out of place was the recipe book near the stove. He leaned over it, opening it where a slip of paper separated the pages.

The pages in the cookbook featured two recipes for fudge cookies and caramel chip cookies. But the slip of paper was a handwritten recipe.

For triple chocolate chip cookies.

"Sorry for taking so long." Maeve's voice made him jerk, dropping his hand so the book slammed shut. Sidling into the room—which was now much too small with her there with him—Maeve opened the fridge, looked inside, then closed it. Turning to him, her cheeks flushed, she said, "I don't have any beer, but I do have some vodka Sally left here the last time she came over. Actually, she invited herself over because Sly was working late and she was bored, and she brought their liquor cabinet with her. All that's left is the vodka."

Forcing himself to move his feet, he slid to the other side of the peninsula separating the kitchen space from a small breakfast nook that abutted the open living room space.

"Vodka's fine." One drink, then he was out. He needed to put more space between them.

She pulled a mug from a cupboard then opened the freezer for the vodka, and turned back to him.

He stared at the mug, confused.

She giggled. "Yeah...I don't have shot glasses, so one of my many mugs will just have to do."

Many? "How many do you have?"

Her flush deepened and she shrugged. "Well, by my last count...seventy."

"Wow."

"Yeah. My addiction to mugs is out of control. I see one that tickles my fancy and I buy it. I know there's no way I can use them all, but they make me happy, so what's the harm?"

...out of control mug collection. Where had he heard that? It was just there, on the tip of his brain. He couldn't quite grab hold of it.

"Here," Maeve said, thrusting a coffee mug into his hands. On the mug was the image of a red pen dripping blood with the words, "Kill Your Darlings," beneath it.

AJ held it up, turning to her with raised eyebrows.

She snickered. "That's one I got from my best friend, Callie. We went to community college together, and we edited and proofread each other's class projects. She said I was a literary serial killer because, when I was done editing her work using my trusty red ink pen, it looked like I murdered it. That quote is from late, great William Faulkner. He says that we should never be afraid to 'kill our darlings' or remove unnecessary words."

Mug of vodka in hand, AJ sat on the loveseat, the cushion beneath him sinking in. Maeve sat on the seat next to him, turning her body until her knee brushed against his. She leaned back and lifted her own mug of vodka to her lips.

The silence in the apartment was heavy with expectation.

Of what, though?

Say something! "Where'd you go to community college?"

She smiled, her face brightening in a way he'd never seen before.

Hard to see much of anything about her when you've spent the last five months comparing her to a small, unobtrusive rodent. Not even bothering to peek over the computer screen and meet her gaze.

And he'd missed out on the bluest eyes he'd ever seen.

adoring **ALEJANDRO**

"Ocala. It's where I met Callie. She was there because she'd gotten pregnant right after high school and she couldn't attend Florida State as she'd planned. I was scared shitless because I was on my own for the first time, and I was never really good at making friends. It was the first morning of my business admin class, and she came right in, sat down next to me, and spent the whole class period trying to keep her eyes open. After class, she admitted that she'd been up all night because her daughter was teething. I felt bad for her, so I gave her my notes. The next day, she brought me a coffee in a travel mug that said, 'Sorry. I'm cranky cuz I missed my nap.' We've been friends ever since."

"The first in your mug collection?"

"No. I'd already been two years deep by then. I still have that travel mug, though. Somewhere."

"Why mugs?"

"Why not?"

"Fair enough."

"What about your family? Are they in Ocala?"

She paused, as if considering how much to share. It didn't escape his notice that, though she'd been working for Harris for five months, and was friends with his sister and Anna, he didn't know much about the woman seated beside him.

"My mom died when I was born, so I don't remember her. My dad remarried when I was seven. I have a step-sister. A few step-cousins. No one I really talk to." From the pained look on her face, AJ knew there was more to it than that. There was a history, a family darkness that he knew and recognized.

Maeve Thomas had a troubled family life.

There was pain there, too. I know what that feels like. What that looks like. Kindred spirits. Spirits that are weighted down with an old pain that cannot be alleviated.

Again, something from Swan's emails pricked at his thoughts, almost like an echo shouted into his mind that only bounced back when he least expected it.

"My mom died seven years ago. It hit Sally the hardest because she was the closest to her."

"What about your dad?"

"He might as well be dead for all I care. The man is a piece of shit, and I'd rather not talk about him."

She paused, then nodded carefully.

"Okay. Why construction?"

AJ didn't know how much time passed as he sat there on the small floral loveseat, sipping vodka from a diabolical coffee mug. He just knew that he hadn't felt as comfortable with a woman in a long time. It just felt natural to sit with Maeve, listening to her talk, laughing with her. Sharing with her. It was like it was something they'd done before, like it was…familiar. Like they'd been doing it forever.

And he didn't want it to stop.

Shards of awareness sliced through him. Realization and remembrance tumbled and collided.

Swan.

He didn't want this with *Maeve*, he wanted it with Swan.

Who also had an out of control mug collection.

With shaking hands, he placed the now empty mug on the coffee table, drawing himself back until his spine was pressed painfully against the arm of the loveseat.

"It's late. I've got to get home."

She glanced at the clock over the TV and offered a guilty smile. "Oh. Yeah, of course. Sorry for keeping you. I didn't mean to bore the hell out of you for so long." She put her mug next to his, the movement making her thigh rub against his.

Immediately, that simple touch sent desire shooting through him, aimed squarely at his cock. Thankfully, he'd grabbed a small pillow earlier on which to rest his aching arms. It was still there, hiding his half-chub from view.

"I wasn't bored. On the contrary, I had a great time talking with you, Maeve. And that's the problem."

"I don't understand. Why would enjoying yourself with me be a problem?"

Heavy silence greeted her question, even as her heart hammered like a drum solo in her ears. Between them, a balloon of heat grew, swelling, nearing to bursting.

His eyes burned with lust, piercing her, tearing the clothes from her body in his mind. The junction between her thighs caught fire, scorching her clit, liquefying her need, and leaking it into her panties.

She wanted him, terribly.

Was the problem that he didn't really want her?

"Is the problem me?" she asked, her voice trembling. "Do you not want me? Am I too fa—"

He grabbed hold of her face and slammed his mouth on to hers. She inhaled sharply, his scent hitting her just as his tongue began teasing the crease of her lips.

"Don't. You are beautiful, so fucking sexy," he growled, frustrated.

She had no idea what to say, what to think. She bit her lip, trying to corral her thoughts, to slow her heartbeat, to cool her need.

But he wasn't having that.

His gaze locked with hers, and she couldn't tear herself

away. Her belly cartwheeling, her heart pounding, her pussy walls clenching and unclenching around nothing.

She needed him to fill her up. Nice and full.

Shivering, she waited.

AJ, forcing her chin up, leaned in and pressed a soft kiss on her lips, leaving her hungry and wanting.

She reached up, grasping his shoulders, silently begging him to draw her near, take her lips again, and feed her his taste.

Finally, his mouth found hers again, and she was lost. Never wanting to be found again. So hot. So good. A ball of pleasure unfurled within her, branching out like the rays of a rising sun. Her body lit up, catching fire.

But the fire quickly died when he jerked away from her, slamming his own hand over his mouth.

She shivered at the loss of his heat, her now empty grip falling into her lap.

"This was a mistake. I…I can't do this with you, Maeve. No matter how much I want to keep going until we're both sweaty and weak from orgasms, I can't do it. Not to you."

"Do *what* to me? I want this, AJ."

"But…I think…I want someone else."

Maeve recoiled as if he'd slapped her. He knew immediately he'd said the wrong thing.

Moaning, he shoved his hands through his hair.

"Not like that, Maeve. I want you, I do. But that's as far as it can go. I…have feelings for another woman, and I feel like doing this, with you, is unfair to her."

He couldn't be sure, but it seemed like understanding then…determination crossed her face. What was that about?

She stood, putting space between them. Space he still didn't even know if he wanted.

Fuck, he was confused and frustrated and fucking horny.

"I understand, AJ. I get it. No hard feelings, okay? We'll just…forget this happened, yeah?"

Swallowing down the immediate response of 'No!', he got to his feet and peered down into her flushed face. Her eyes had hardened, no longer the desire softened blue orbs. They were now glinting and steely.

He'd hurt her, he knew he did, but there was nothing he could do about it now.

"Yeah," he finally responded. He headed toward the door. She didn't follow him, remaining in front of the loveseat, her unreadable gaze on him. His hand on the doorknob, he hesitated. He didn't want to leave. He wanted to stay. With her. To finish what they started.

But Swan…she deserved more. And, up until that night at Velvet, he'd wanted to give it to her. How had everything gotten so twisted and fucked?

"Goodnight, Maeve," he breathed, unable to tear his gaze from hers.

She offered him a flimsy smile. "See you tomorrow, boss."

Boss.

A blatant reminder of what he was to her. She was rebuilding that wall that he'd smashed through when he stole that first kiss…then second.

With a pathetic wave, he opened the door and slid through it.

He flinched at the sound of the lock clicking into place on the other side, like the click of a trigger on a gun, pointed straight at his chest.

From the Desk of SWAN

December 5th

AJ, my love, I'm sorry that I've been slow to respond. My only excuse is that I'm scared. I'm scared of where this is going, and how deep it's gotten. When I first wrote to you, I could only dream that you would eventually feel the same way for me that I feel for you. For that to be a reality this quickly feels surreal. Like it cannot possibly be true. I'm terrified that I love you so much and that someday I'll lose you. That the day we finally meet...you'll walk away.

I know you think that you love me enough that you don't care what I look like, but that hasn't been my experience. All my life, people have looked at me and judged me unfairly.

But...I am willing to offer you something of me. I am braving the unknown and stepping out into the real world. I can't promise that I'll walk right up to you and throw my arms around you like I so desperately want to do, but I can promise that I will give this "real life" thing a shot.

When? I don't know. Sometime soon, I hope. Just continue being patient with me, please. I promise, it will be worth the wait.

Love, your Swan.

PS. I'm glad you enjoyed the cookies. It only took me three tries to get the recipe right.

chapter
EIGHT

When Swan said she'd give the "real life" thing a shot, that she was braving the unknown to step out and meet him, AJ couldn't have imagined it would happen so soon.

He hurried toward conference room B on the third floor of the White Estate Corporation building, the glittering lights of downtown Miami lighting his way down the darkened corridor. The rest of the holiday party—the music, the booze, and the people—were all on the first floor in the building's large open atrium. The party, a glitzy, extravagant affair, was a gift from billionaire boss, Sylvester White—his future brother-in-law if that man had anything to say about it, and a man with more money than taste. The only reason AJ had attended was because someone from Harris Construction, LLC had to be present at the party to rub elbows and kiss asses.

Since Blaze, his best friend and partner, was busy making merry with his new fiancée, Anna, it left AJ holding the bag and the plane ticket to Miami for the weekend. It wasn't that he hated flying or doing the hob-knobbing for business sake, it was the falseness and consumerism of the holiday season that soured his mood. And it didn't help that, once again, it was just him, alone, on his own for Christmas. Sure, he could celebrate with his sister Sallina—he wouldn't be alone then. But that wasn't the sort of alone that needed fixing. He'd always have Sallina, and now Sylvester. He also had Blaze and Anna. Two couples. To him, they were his two brothers and two sisters. And their lives were full of love and commitment, with a future that promised more blessings than AJ could ever know. Would ever know. Because he didn't have what they had…but God, he wanted it. Had been hoping, praying for it—*craving* it—for years.

And now, he just might have it.

Five minutes ago, a waiter dressed in coattails and starched, white shirt handed him a folded note, a note the waiter said had been handed to him by a woman, a message that had turned the depressing party on its fucking head.

IF YOU WANT TO MEET ME, COME TO THE 3RD FLOOR, CONF. RM. B. DON'T SPEAK. KEEP THE LIGHTS OFF. I AM WAITING FOR YOU.

It wasn't signed, but he knew who it was. It was the

woman who'd been taunting him, seducing him, enticing him for the last four months. And he was more than damn well ready to solve the mystery of the woman he'd never seen but couldn't get out of his head.

But no more! Now the mystery would be solved. Now he would know who was behind the emails, gifts, and long nights of blue balls and cold showers. He would finally put a face and body to the words that kept him up at night, made him smile and laugh, filled his chest with terrible longing, and eased the loneliness that had been eating away at him for years. A loneliness that no amount of flirting or fucking, one-night stands, and disappointing dates could abate.

From that first email, he'd been intrigued. So much so that other women paled in comparison to his gut-twisting interest in a woman he couldn't even completely picture in his mind. Was she tall or short, butterscotch or chocolate, curvy or svelte, blonde or brunette or ginger? What color were her eyes? Did they twinkle when she laughed? Did she have freckles, a beauty mark, a fucking dimple? What did she look like when she smiled? Did her grin light up the room, did it turn heads, did it bring men to their knees? What did she sound like? Was her voice lyrical or husky? What did she smell like? Citrus or flowers? Vanilla or cinnamon? Most importantly...what would see feel like under his eager hands? What would it be like to pull her into his arms and hold her? What would her lips feel like pressed against his? What would she taste like as he devoured her—*all* of her?

Over and over, on repeat, those questions cascaded through his mind, and the utter lack of answers was driving him insane.

Four months of celibacy was difficult, not impossible, but definitely painful. In an effort to prove to himself that he was still a red-blooded male, that he hadn't lost his mind falling for a probable catfish scheme, he'd hit the bars with a few guys from work, flirting with the beautiful, beachy women who'd frequented places like Happy Jack's and Anchors. He'd smile, sidle up to buy her a drink, and she'd touch him—and he'd balk. The very thought of another woman's hands on him made his skin crawl, his stomach knot, and his cock deflate.

Except Maeve. You love her hands all over you.

Gritting his teeth, he attempted to push her from his mind for the umpteenth time just that day. He was minutes from meeting Swan—Maeve shouldn't even be a blip in his mind at that moment.

Nothing about this was normal. But right then, he didn't give a shit. He was going to meet Swan, touch her, and finally—*finally!*—put a face and body to the fantasies that kept him awake and hard all night, every night.

Turning down the long corridor toward the conference rooms, his stride eating the distance, the note burning a hole in his pocket, AJ's heart pounded, his chest heaved, his mind spun. So close.

Closer.

There. Conference room B. No windows were looking in from the corridor, only a single door. One door between him and his Swan. She'd chosen this room well…which meant she was familiar with this building. He'd known all along she had to work for Sylvester. There were too many clues in their correspondence, and she'd often mention seeing him or hearing about him. So, he knew she was an employee—which did little to narrow down the prospects. There were fifty people alone in the White offices in Jackson Key, and the White offices in Miami had closer to 500. And since AJ often visited the Miami office on errands for Sylvester or Blaze, he came in contact with women from the Miami office at least three times a month. Any one of the hundreds of women working for White could be the woman standing behind the door. In the dark. Waiting for him.

Go inside.

He was shaking, his blood ravaging through him, his cock already hard and aching—because he was damned if he left that room without tasting her.

One taste.

No! That wouldn't be enough. Not after all he'd suffered—not after all she'd put him through. Tonight, he would finally know what she looked like, smelled like, tasted like, and how it felt to press his body against hers. How it felt to be inside her.

She's right here.

The note said to keep the lights off. That meant it was dark inside. That meant she was probably hoping to keep her identity a secret. But for how much longer? And how did she plan to keep him from touching her or hearing her voice? Yeah, her note told him not to speak, but what about her? How could they possibly meet without seeing or speaking?

Fuck that. He'd find a way. And, besides, there was always touching. He couldn't wait to put his hands on her, know the texture of her flesh, the shape of her body, the sounds she made when he finally slid his hands over her skin, cupped her face…kissed her mouth.

I bet she tastes like the mocha coffee she keeps talking about in her emails; the mocha chocolate lattes she says she cannot go a morning without. No matter what, AJ knew she would taste better than anything he'd ever put in his mouth…or ever would. The thought of her taste alone made him drag in a shuddering breath, his lungs refusing to work even as he'd powered across the carpeted floor toward the rendezvous point.

But why was she hiding in the dark? Was she scared he wouldn't like what he saw? Was she shy? Or did she just want to drag out the tension, the eroticism of sensory deprivation?

Perhaps she liked a good, hard fuck in the dark.

Does it really matter? She's right there on the other side of the door. You've wanted this for four months!

What was stopping him from walking into the room and turning on the light despite her words in the letter?

He knew the answer before the words wholly formed in his mind.

Trust.

He wanted Swan to trust him. To him, trust was as important as love. Without one, you couldn't have the other—not in its purity, anyway. How many marriages fell apart because trust was gone? How many people vowed before God and their loved ones that they could be trusted with the person standing across from them at the altar? And how many of those people didn't deserve the trust placed in them? How many divorces? And in the case of his parents, how many marriages were nightmares cloaked in pretty, glittering opulence over a decaying, rotten tomb?

Yes, he could walk into the room and turn on the lights, uncovering the mystery of who Swan was with the flick of a light switch, but he knew in his gut that would be the end of things. Forever. She'd feel betrayed, run from him, and never speak to him again.

And he'd rather swallow a real sword than hurt her. His Swan.

What about speaking? Asking her questions? He knew

the letter asked him to remain silent, but shouldn't there be some conversation? An introduction—a real one? He could do that, but...something kept him in place. Something he couldn't wrap his mind around.

Why the smoke and mirrors?

Why the mystery at all? In this day and age, women were empowered, fierce, taking life and men by the balls. They didn't need to hide behind technology and secrets to get what they wanted—and Swan wanted him. Her words—from whimsical to sweet to sexy—had been all about her attraction to him, how much she wanted him, how much she wanted more with him. And he'd eaten them up with a spoon.

After spending eighteen years witnessing the ugly side of marriage between his parents, the side where the dutiful, faithful wife stayed true to a diabolical, sadist, cheating asshole of a husband, AJ knew he wanted better for himself. He knew that the woman his mother had been was a beautiful, rare kind of woman: faithful even through the most terrible pain, even to the point of self-destruction. And he wanted a woman like that—less the destruction part. He craved, needed, yearned to find a woman who would love him, adore him, remain faithful to him even when he was an asshole, as—to be completely honest—most men could be at least sixty percent of the time. And, in return, he would be the kind of husband a jewel like her deserved. Just as faithful, just as adoring and loving, and protective and possessive and passionate. AJ was ready and eager to be a husband, to share his life with a woman who epitomized his dream... and she was no more than a few feet away, waiting in a conference room for him to arrive.

His Swan. His dream woman.

adoring ALEJANDRO

And he would damn well make this amazing woman his forever. If he could find a way to get her out of the shadows and into his arms for good.

Now, it appeared that she'd finally decided it was time to come out from hiding, at least from behind a computer screen. She was finally giving him a chance to be with her—the woman he could see himself falling in love with. She was a swan, not a mouse.

Suddenly, an image of Maeve slammed into his mind. Her lips swollen from his kisses, her face flushed with desire, her blue eyes alight with a fire he'd also felt racing through his blood. She'd been like sensual perfection, her lush curves pressed against his hardness.

But she was off limits. His employee. His sister's friend.

He shook his head, determined to dislodge the memories of that moment in her office when he'd lost his fucking head and kissed her. And then, that night in her apartment, when they'd talked like best friends then kissed like lust-drowned lovers. Maeve was a gorgeous, desirable woman. A woman who wasn't Swan.

He quickly squashed the guilt that surfaced, because he couldn't meet his woman for the first time with thoughts of Maeve—and what they'd done—taking up any space in his head.

Here's your chance. Take it!

Raising his hand, he knocked once, signaling his arrival. He didn't want to scare her.

From beyond the door, a muffled, feminine voice called, "Come in," sending tongues of fire through his blood. He shuddered, his large body shaking with anticipation.

Sucking in a breath, AJ opened the door.

chapter
NINE

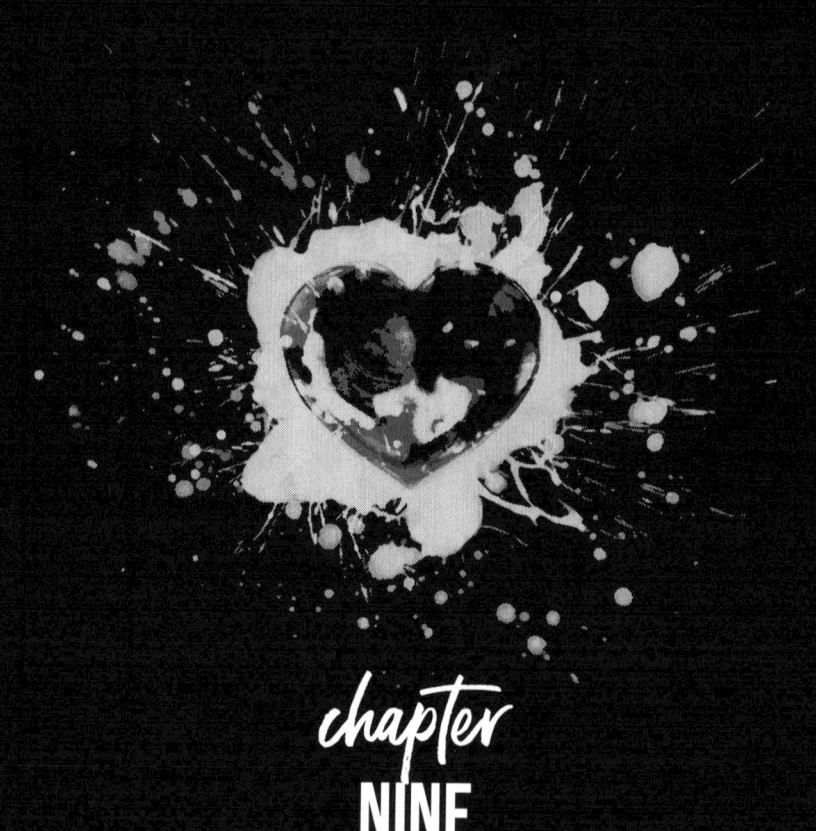

OH GOD, HE'S HERE! HE'S ACTUALLY HERE! WHAT THE *hell am I doing?*

Yup, she was crazy. Absolutely, out of her mind, padded room crazy.

But it was too late to lock herself away and throw away the key, because the man she'd been falling in love with for the last six months was standing on the other side of the door, waiting for her response to his knock.

Her mouth, which was obviously not connected to her brain, opened, and called, "Come in!"

Dammit! She wasn't ready! Was she? The room she'd chosen was a small conference room. There were no windows, so without the light on, it was perfectly pitch black inside. There was a single conference table, six chairs, and nothing else. The added bonus of the room was that there were two doors, one that opened from the corridor where AJ was standing, and another leading to the junior executive offices, which were locked down at night. She'd planned for this. She'd wanted the chance to be with AJ…but she also wanted an escape route just in case something went wrong. If the 'wrong' did happen, she could hurry herself right out the other door, locking it behind her. He'd never know who she was…and she'd be safe. To wallow in unrequited love's misery forever.

This is your only chance! Take it!

Not that she had a choice, since the door was opening, casting a beam of light across the conference room table to her left. She'd positioned herself in the corner, knowing the light from the corridor would follow AJ in, and wanting to remain hidden for as long as she could. The dark was her friend.

She watched, her heart hammering, as AJ large frame slipped through the opening. Slowly, he closed the door behind him, the door latch clicking into place.

Only the sound of their breathing—fast and ragged— could be heard.

Finally, after long, pounding seconds, he spoke. "Hello? Why's it dark in here?" he asked, his deep voice carrying through the dark and right into her pussy.

Crazy. She was crazy. But she was also desperate! She couldn't live her life watching and wondering. She'd done that for far too long. She was done with being the invisible nobody everyone ignored—especially the man she'd fallen in love with.

"You're speaking," she rasped, her faux accent in place.

Yes, she realized that fooling him by playing a part wasn't going to make the big reveal any easier, but she convinced herself that she just needed some time to speak with him in person without him knowing who she really was. They'd chat face to face—even though they couldn't see one another—he'd fall in love with her, and once the lights came on, he wouldn't care that she was his plump, plain, shy office manager. "You aren't supposed to speak."

He chuckled. "So I am. I'm not sorry, though. Does that mean you won't speak with me? That you'll stay hiding in the dark?"

"I'm only in the dark because I am not quite ready to… officially *meet*," she replied weakly. Lord, she was treading on dangerous grounds. All he had to do was reach over and hit the light switch—her plans would be blasted to smithereens, and he'd probably laugh in her face…right after he ripped her a new one for fooling him. Then, he'd probably fire her.

She sucked in a breath, panic rushing through her.

After her rescue and then their make out session on her loveseat, Maeve had been emboldened to finally take the next step. To come out from behind the screen and make the next move. Their kiss had been molten, setting them both on fire. But he'd stopped them.

Because he wanted to remain faithful to Swan.

To *her*. Maeve. His obvious frustration and guilt were unnecessary because the two women he was caught between were the same person.

Her first feeling was immense guilt. It was her fault he was so torn up. But she could alleviate his guilt with a simple sentence.

I am Swan.

When she'd realized that, she'd nearly admitted she was

Swan right then and there, but she knew dumping that on him in that heated moment would have caused a chain reaction and blown up in both their faces. No. She needed the time to figure out how to slowly and carefully reveal herself as Swan. And AJ needed time to come down from the lust and vexation he was feeling. He'd been tense as a fully drawn bowstring, and Maeve knew that revealing the truth right then would have made him snap.

She loved him. She didn't want to hurt him.

Yeah, like lying to him for the last four months hasn't been hurting him. The man was a twisted knot thanks to Swan's emails and Maeve's actions—kissing him and practically begging him to fuck her. But how was she supposed to know that AJ would actually be attracted to her as Maeve? For months, he'd looked through her, and for years before that, she'd been the ugly, fat, nobody everyone sneered at. What were the chances that a man as gorgeous and sexually experienced as AJ, a man surrounded by gorgeous women in bikinis—it was a small beach town after all—would actually feel anything for her other than friendliness. She was still stunned by the fact that he'd been the one to kiss her first. AJ desired her. Fat and all.

Because of her actions, however, AJ was confused, and a man of action like AJ, thrived on clarity.

It was time to make things perfectly clear. Well, as clear as they could be in a dark conference room. She told herself that she just needed one final step before the big reveal to ease herself into it. Because once it was out there, once AJ knew for certain that mousy, chubby Maeve was the enigmatic Swan, there was no taking it back. He could either bypass anger and go right to ecstatic, or he could feel betrayed, slighted, and hate her forever.

EVE BLACK

Either way, tonight was the beginning of the end of her charade. If she didn't puke first.

A heavy sigh filled the silence left by her retreat into her thoughts.

"So, we're to meet in the dark? How does that work? I want to see you. I want to touch you. This isn't what I was expecting when I got your note." Irritation and disappointment colored his words, and she felt the mood in the room shift. If she didn't do something soon, he'd leave, and that would be the end of everything.

Dragging in a quiet breath, she made sure her faux accent was in place then admitted, "I'm scared. I have no idea what I am doing. I know you want to see me, and I want you to…just not yet."

"What is it? What are you hiding from me? Are you scared that I won't like what I see?"

Of course, someone was smart as AJ would figure it out.

It wasn't all that hard, dumbass. You're hiding from him—in the same room!

"Honestly, yes."

He choked on a laugh and she felt him move…closer. It was like the heat and scent of him grew more intense. He was only a few feet away now, instead of by the door. Now that their eyes had adjusted, she could easily make out his outline, which meant he could do the same for her…if she stepped away from the conference room table she was leaning against. It served a dual purpose: it helped her orient herself in the dark, and it helped keep her upright, since her legs were useless jelly.

"So…what are you wearing?" AJ asked, a teasing yet curious note in his voice.

Maeve snickered. "Something slinky, if a bit Christmassy. Must dress for the season and situation, you know."

He chuckled.

"What are *you* wearing?" What's good for the goose….

"Well, I didn't even really want to come to this party, but I had to represent, you know. You could just let me turn on the light, and you can see for yourself. My sister says I look dashing in a tux."

God, did she want to see that. She wanted to turn on the lights, get an eyeful of sexy as fuck AJ in a tux, but she wasn't quite ready for him to get an eyeful of her.

"Light stays off. For now."

"So, this is a *blind* date, huh?" he said, humor in his voice this time. A smidgeon of relief helped to lessen the tension roiling between them. She smothered a laugh.

"I suppose so, yes. It was also supposed to be a silent date."

He chuckled…and moved closer. She could feel him standing within reach. At any time, she could reach out and touch him—really touch him. Just as she wanted to. Without fearing disgusted or leering looks. She could touch him, place her hand upon him and feel the hardness of his muscles beneath her palm. She could trace the lines of his chest and torso with her fingers, running them along each ridge of his abs, over the slab of his pecs. She swallowed.

She *could* touch.

So she did, slowly running her fingers over his chest. He rumbled, groaning at her touch. Her body responded, heating, flooding her with need. Feeling her way from his bowtie to his belt buckle, she experienced the most intense physical tease of her life.

She raised her second hand, trailing her fingertips along

his exposed neck, up around to the back of his head to thread her hand into his thick, silky hair.

At her touch, he hissed, sucking in a sharp breath.

"Fuck," he grunted. "You're touching me, Swan. Your hands…they're on me." He sounded pained, as though her hands were causing him agony. She dropped her hands. "No!" he barked, making her jump. "Put them back, don't ever stop touching me."

She did…then moaned. God, he was like living, breathing steel. Hot. Hard.

Heat coursed through her, replacing her blood with lava, filling her core with liquid need. She pressed her thighs together, hoping to stave off the desire to rub her pussy against him…or beg him to touch her back.

But he couldn't touch her. He'd figure out pretty quickly that she wasn't the thin, sexy woman he probably imagined her as.

"You-you can touch me," she offered, reaching up to grip his hard, broad shoulders. From there, she ran her seeking hands down his thick biceps, to his forearms, to his large hands. Taking his hands, she lifted them, placing them against her neck.

"From here up, touch as you like."

He tensed. There, in the darkness and lusty haze, all she could hear was the sounds of their breathing. His breaths were slow, almost thoughtful.

"Still hiding from me, Swan," was all he said, before he cupped her face and groaned. "I'll take what I can get," he murmured, his voice like smoke and fire. "For now."

chapter TEN

Beneath his hands was the softest, silkiest skin he'd ever felt in his life. Her panting breaths fluttered over his eyes and cheeks and mouth. He could smell the cherry and vanilla on her breath, like she had a delicious treat right before slipping into the room.

Just like he was about to have a delicious treat.

He leaned in, closing his eyes. He wanted to feel everything, right down to the ends of the hairs on his arms where her hands were holding him. When she'd said to keep his hands on her face, she'd meant it.

She was truly scared of revealing too much—or much of anything at all. But that wouldn't matter in the long run.

Soon, he would convince her that she had nothing to fear, that he was attracted to her soul.

And that convincing started with a kiss.

"I'm going to kiss you now, my Swan," he breathed, the sensation of his lips brushing against hers made them both gasp softly. Damn, that sound made his body tighten, heat pooling in his groin, scorching through him until all nerve endings were raw and throbbing. That's what she'd sound like beneath him as he explored her body with his tongue.

"Yes, please kiss me," she whimpered.

In the dark, in the silence, he was blind only in sight, but he body could feel hers, his nose could smell her arousal, the scent of cherries and vanilla on her breath. Leaning in, closer…closer…until his lips brushed against hers again.

"Magic…" he whispered, then pressed his lips against hers again, harder, sucking her top lip in between his. Slowly, he tasted her. Cherry vanilla. Delectable.

Digging his fingers into the back of her head, he deepened the kiss, using lips and teeth to entice, enthrall, enslave, until she gasped, panting.

Then, he devoured. His tongue slid into the cavern of her mouth, owning it, taking, invading. She was timid at first, holding back, keeping a part of herself from him.

Fuck that, he wanted it all.

Using his thumbs, he held her jaw in place, forcing her to engage, to draw as he pushed, to pull as he gave, and they kissed and hungered and thirsted and quenched that thirst with one another.

His body was alive, strumming like a guitar with strings so tight one single stroke would make him snap.

Drawing back to nip her bottom lip, he breathed over

her swollen lips, "You are killing me, baby." Trembling against him, she moaned. "Let me touch you, please."

He was begging. Because he desperately to feel her flesh beneath his twitching, eager hands.

He could feel her shake her head, her silky hair sliding between his fingers.

"N-no, you can't," she husked, her breathing labored as his was. "I'm not ready."

Not yet, anyway.

"I'll take what I can get, then," he growled, slamming his mouth on to hers again.

Ravenous.

So fucking turned on, his cock was throbbing, precum leaking from the tip. Every movement, every tweak of muscle, vibrated through him to his painfully erect dick.

Forcing his every need into his kiss, he deepened it.

Ferocious in his desire for her, he feasted.

A loud clatter then a shout tore through the room, shattering the moment. Making them jump apart like two magnets with opposing poles. Terror surged. Someone was coming. Something or someone hit the wall just beside the door to the room where she was standing, vulnerable, with the man who could tear her world apart.

He wouldn't. After that kiss, he'd be happy to know Swan is you.

But she couldn't know that for sure.

Another loud bump against the wall. Much closer.

So much for the third floor being deserted.

Whoever they are, they probably had the same idea as you.

AJ swore, and she could feel him pulling away and turning toward the door.

He was going to open the door, turn on the light.

Reveal her and all her secrets.

No! She wasn't ready!

Survival instinct kicked in. The hairs on her arms stood up straight, and the heat and desire from the kiss turned to *flight*.

She had to get out of there.

Turning, she placed her hand on the table beside her and used it as a guide to the other door on the other side of the room. She moved as fast as she could in the dark.

Behind her, AJ cursed again.

"Who's in there? Y-you hav-havin' schex in-in there?" A high pitched male giggle sounded, only increasing her panic. The doorknob jiggled as the man shouted, "Let us in, we can join you!"

"Dammit," AJ grumbled into the darkness. "I'm sorry, baby, but I've got to turn the light on. These clowns need to go."

No. Just a few more seconds.

She nearly cried out in relief when she felt the coolness of the doorknob in her grip. Quick as she could, she turned the knob and yanked the door open, hurrying through it just as the light flicked on behind her. Yanking the door shut, she made sure it was locked, then practically tripped over her own feet as she stumbled backward until her back hit the wall across the corridor.

On the other side of the door there was muffled conversation, a raised voice, then silence.

Then, "Fuck! Where did she go?"

She could hear the pounding of his feet as he ran to

the door right in front of her. The door she locked so he couldn't follow.

The knob turned then jerked. Then rattled violently. Then he pounded his fist against the wood.

"Goddammit, no! Swan! Swan, baby!"

Tears of guilt and agony streamed down her cheeks.

God, she was such a fool. Such a cowardly fool.

More muffled cursing, then one final fist pound on the door, this one so hard it rattled the walls.

In a voice heavy with grief and disappointment, AJ murmured, "Why did she run? What did I do?"

You didn't do anything! This is all me, all my fault. You were perfect, amazing…and I love you.

She couldn't feel herself moving until she was already where she desperately needed to be.

"Fuck this shit," AJ spat, anger like a knife cutting through her soul.

Don't be angry. It wasn't you…it was me. But rather than say those words to the man she loved, she simply stood there on the other side of the locked door, her trembling hand pressed against the wood.

Listening to his retreat, she and cried.

From the Desk of AJ Mendez

December 18th,

You taste like cherries. Cherry is my new favorite flavor. Your lips my new favorite thing. So soft. Perfect. I could have kissed you for the rest of my life.

Why did you run? We were just getting started, baby. I have to admit, you leaving like that made me angry, but then I remembered you admitting your fear, that you were scared.

I don't understand that fear because I know, in my heart, that there's nothing about you that will change my feelings. But I will be patient, waiting for you to be ready. To find your strength.

But how long will that be, Swan?

When can I taste you again?

When can I see you? To be so close to you, to not get to touch you like I needed to, to not talk to you like I wanted to...it was a tease. A delicious tease. I know turning on the light was a risk, but after that kiss you have to have known how I feel about you. That I don't give a fuck what you look like because I am attracted to your heart, your soul, and your kisses.

You were so fucking sexy, baby. No, I didn't see

you, but to hear your voice, to drag your scent into my nose, to feel your body heat, was the sexiest experience of my life. I've been as hard as steel since then. Next time we meet, all the lights will be on, so I can see you as I make you come.

Please, don't leave me waiting much longer.

Forever yours,

AJ

P.S. If I don't see you before Christmas...Merry Christmas.

chapter
ELEVEN

He was running late, but it couldn't be helped. After not getting a single wink of sleep the night before, he'd sat and stared at his phone, waiting for Swan's response to his email from Sunday. Without sleep, he'd fallen behind on his usual morning routine. More like nuked it. Exercise, shower, coffee, then head to the office. Today, though, his workout was ruined because he couldn't get his cock to go down. Ever try to run with a cockstand? His shower was ruined because no matter how cold the water, his blood still boiled inside him, just like the come in his balls, eager to pump from his dick and into Swan's willing body. Because he was already behind, he couldn't rub one out like he wanted to, not that fucking his own hand would even begin to sate his need for the woman who ran from him like her hair was on fire. His coffee was more bitter than normal, and the drive to work was clogged with last minute Christmas shoppers crowding the roads.

He'd hoped that two days was sufficient enough time for her to calm down and reach out to him. Still nothing.

After their clandestine meet up at White, AJ had spent the rest of the evening scouring every face at the party, looking for her. No, he had no idea what she looked like, but from how he had to bend down to kiss her, he could approximate her height as somewhere between five-foot-four and five-foot-seven. Unless she'd been wearing heels, which could throw him off by several inches.

She also smelled like cherry vanilla, a scent he'd never associated with sex before, but now he couldn't not. Just the memory of that scent in his nostrils and that taste on his tongue made his mouth water to taste and smell her again. To drag the scent of Swan and sensuality into his lungs and absorb it into his bloodstream. Make her a part of him, right to his cells.

He pulled up and parked his truck beside a BMW he'd never seen before. It was probably a client coming to sign some paperwork. It wouldn't be the first time. Grabbing his beat-up leather satchel with projects plans and documents in it, and his nearly empty travel mug, he headed toward the small building where Blaze was waiting to have their Monday morning meeting.

Maeve would be in, too. She was always there, bright and early. Up until the last few weeks, though, he'd never given her much thought outside of her just…being there. Being useful. As an employee of Harris Construction.

Now, though, after kissing her twice, and foolishly acknowledging the attraction between them, he noticed and anticipated so much more.

And that was what was tearing him the fuck up. Maeve and Swan. Two different women, two different circumstances, but the level of utter need for each of them was the same. What he felt for Swan seemed… heavy, needful, his heart and mind both engaged. But with Maeve, it was his heart, mind, and body—as though each part of him was waking up for the first time after he'd thrust them into dreamless slumber years ago.

He could thank his cheating, asshole father for that. He'd learned early to lock up all the vulnerable parts of himself, to keep safe and sane.

Loneliness and emptiness had taken the place of hope and love.

He was changing that.

But wait—after Friday night at the holiday party….

His body hardened, his muscles tensing at the mere memory of his flesh against Swan's. His devouring mouth against her soft, succulent, submissive lips. She gave as he took, and he'd never felt such incredible hunger as he had in that moment.

Except when he was kissing Maeve.

Fuck.

Apparently, he was enough like his father to be attracted to more than one woman. He hadn't cheated, technically, but he was still emotionally and now physically involved with two women.

Lifting his head, he spotted someone getting out of the BMW. Long blonde hair, a tight, tailored sweater dress that hugged a frame that was more at home on the catwalk than a construction office parking lot. The blonde turned, bright red lips smiling at him.

"Denise?" Fuck. What she was she doing there? Hadn't she gotten the hint from his non-responses to her calls and texts that he wasn't interested? Shit. "What are you doing here?" *At my place of work* and *in my goddamn town?*

"Hello, AJ," she purred, her lips spreading into a wicked smile. He supposed a normal man would be drawn in by an inviting smile like that, but he wasn't normal. His current fucked up situation was proof of that.

As she came around her car to stand before him, he steeled himself. Women like Denise would take any sign they could that you were interested, so he turned himself in a block of ice.

"Did I forget a meeting?" Like hell he did. While the woman was gorgeous and gave off hot sex vibes, she also gave off stage five clinger vibes as well. Like she was just waiting for the chance to latch on and suck him dry.

She laughed, raising a hand to press against her chest, trying to draw his attention to the tits pushed together and up in her just barely appropriate daytime attire. "Oh, no, nothing like that. I just thought that…after Friday night…we could finally meet. Face to face."

What the hell was she talking about? Friday night was the holiday party, and he hadn't seen her there. Had actually been hoping to avoid her. Thankfully, he had.

"Friday night? That was the party. Were you there?"

Pouting, she dropped her hand and made a fist. Huffing, she said, "How can you forget so quickly, AJ? It was only the best kiss of my life."

His heart stalled, then tripped over itself to race.

EVE BLACK

His mouth was dry as a desert, his tongue suddenly thick and useless.

Kiss? Denise? He hadn't kissed Denise on Friday night, he'd fucking remember that.

Denise slid her hand up his chest, fingering the collar of his work polo. Leaning in, her breasts brushed against torso. He was a man, a physical, red-blooded male. And his body responded despite what his mind was doing. Which was blanking…then spinning. In successive, jumpy movements.

"I can see you're having difficulty wrapping your head around it, my darling. But I promise you, it was me in that conference room. It was *my* lips you kissed."

Impossible. Swan was *not* Denise. They weren't even in the same ballpark of personalities. For one, Swan had said she was socially awkward. Denise was a mako shark.

But why would she lie? And how would she know about Swan, the conference room, or their kiss if she wasn't who she was claiming to be?

Gathering the last dregs of his sense, he forced a smile. "You're Swan?"

She blushed, nodding coyly.

He couldn't understand it, and didn't have the mental capacity in that moment to try and unwind the confusion from the uncertainty.

She's Swan. It had to be her. Right?

He'd figure out the why and how later.

Grinning and feeling like things just might be falling into place, AJ cupped her face in his hands, bent down, and kissed her.

adoring ALEJANDRO

Denise Walters.

Director of IT for White Estate Corporation.

Blonde Bombshell with the perfect figure, long legs, tight body, perky tits, big blue eyes, and a mouth like Angelina Jolie. She was gorgeous. Smart.

And a raging bitch.

Maeve had the unfortunate pleasure of dealing with Denise when they both worked close to Sly before Sly and Maeve's move to Jackson Key. Maeve had been Sly's newly hired PA, and Denise was the sexual vulture, circling over Sly's head when rumors of his divorce from his wife, Loni, began surfacing. Wherever Sly was, Denise was there, offering her time, attention, and—with little subtly—her body.

Thankfully, the man had better taste than that, but a scorned Denise was a Disney Villain Denise. She took out her vitriol on her whole department, not that Sly could do anything about it, since her barbs hit all the fleshy bits on the inside where people couldn't see.

As Sly's PA, Maeve got her fair share of Denise's rage, but she was finally able to escape when Sly permanently moved the Jackson Key building projects' business to Jackson Key, rather than simply monitoring them from Miami as they'd done on all other projects before. They'd packed up that portion of the business and moved it to Jackson Key, and remained there, out of Denise Walters' reach.

Apparently, their reprieve was over.

Her office was in Miami with the other White execs, so what was she doing in Jackson Key? What was she doing in the Harris Construction office?

Why was she grinning at AJ like he was a prize she'd just scored, and why was *he* looking at *her* like she'd just dropped a nuclear bomb on his head? And he liked it?

"Blaze, hey brother," AJ called, grabbing hold of Denise's hand to drag her behind him as he hurried toward Blaze's office, his smile getting bigger all the time.

Dread crept along her spine, slithering into her chest.

What was happening?

Her gaze dropped to where their hands were clasped together, their fingers woven as lovers would do. Her heart, which had stuttered to a stop at the sight of Denise trailing AJ through the office doors began to pound.

She wanted to open her mouth and ask what was going on, but she didn't. The lump in her throat had grown two sizes, cutting off her air and her voice.

"I told you, man, I told you she was real," AJ boasted, pulling Denise into his side to throw an arm around her shoulders. She snuggled in to him, placing a thinly fingered hand against his sculpted chest.

Maeve's eyes failed her. That had to be what was happening, because just two days ago, AJ was hers. He was kissing *her*! He was touching *her*! He was begging to see her face and spend time with her without all the shadows and emails.

What the hell happened over the weekend that had turned everything upside down?

"Who's this?" Blaze asked, standing up and coming around his desk to stand before the cuddling couple.

AJ's face brightened, his gorgeous emerald eyes shining so bright Maeve could see it from where she was sitting at her desk.

She held her breath, knowing deep in her gut, that AJ's answer would cut her wide open.

"This is her—Swan! The woman I've been emailing with the last four months. This is the woman I've been waiting for my whole life."

What? That's impossible! I'm right here, not over there. More importantly, she wasn't Denise! Denise wasn't her! What the hell was happening?

Her chest constricting, Maeve must have made a noise because the trio turned to look at her. Blaze's eyes flicked to her, AJ's eyes glanced in her direction but didn't meet her gaze, and Denise's eyes…they narrowed, a diabolical venom glimmering in their depths. The smile on her face twisting from faux pleasantry to all too real malice.

That woman knew the truth. And she was wallowing in Maeve's misery.

"Are you serious?" Blaze asked, incredulous, his eyes wide. Wariness and shock flashed in his eyes, and his mouth drew into a hard line. "I didn't think she was real."

AJ laughed, but it was the laugh he used with potential clients. Not the laugh he used with his friends. With her.

"She's here. This is Denise Walters," AJ said, throwing Blaze a look Maeve couldn't read, and she didn't think she wanted to.

"*The* Denise? The one from the Miami office?" The surprise and sharp disbelief in Blaze's voice made Denise shift, her expression becoming guarded.

Oh, yeah, the man isn't fooled by your serpent's smile.

"That's me," the viper bubbled, giving Blaze a wide grin.

He narrowed his eyes, crossing his arms.

"Come on, man, give us a break, yeah?" AJ cautioned, his body tense, his arm around Denise flexing as though he was forcing himself to remain there.

Was he not as sure about Denise as he sounded?

What does it matter? Either way that woman is not you! You have to do something.

She stood, pushing back her desk chair, but the look AJ threw at her made her stop in her tracks. The coldness in his eyes…the clenching of his jaw….

He was telling her to keep her mouth shut and mind her own business.

The look on Denise's face was one of victory.

Maeve sucked in a breath and held it, willing the burning tears behind her eyes to go away. Crying in front of AJ or Denise would only make things worse—she'd look like an idiot, weeping for no apparent reason. Because AJ had no idea what Denise had just done.

Denise smirked, AJ turned away from her, and everything holding Maeve together crumbled to pieces.

chapter TWELVE

THE URGE TO SLAM HER OFFICE DOOR SHUT PUSHED the blood into her extremities, but…she just couldn't do it. Like a train wreck, she couldn't watch but she couldn't look away, either.

The train wreck being her heart and hopes and dreams.

The conversation between Blaze, AJ, and the harpy life-stealer went on for long, agonizing minutes, as AJ introduced Denise and Blaze, then asked for the rest of the day off so he could spend it with her.

"Okay, baby," AJ said, grinning down at Denise. "I need to have this meeting with Blaze really quick, then you and I can spend the day together. How does that sound?" AJ asked, gripping her hips to pull her into him, where she melted against his chest.

That was *her* chest that bitch was touching. That was *her* man!

What the hell was happening? She couldn't just blurt out that Denise was a liar, could she? But if she did, all the effort she'd put in to slowly revealing the truth would be bust. Then again, if she didn't, Denise would get away with whatever the hell she was doing, and AJ would end up with the wrong woman.

She was Swan, she was the one who was supposed to be draped over AJ's gorgeous, hard chest.

"That's okay, baby. I understand. My showing up here is a surprise. But I'd love to spend the day with you. We can grab brunch…maybe…go back to your place." Denise dragged a finger from AJ's mouth, down his throat, and to his pec, grinning up at him suggestively.

The fucker grinned back, heat filling his eyes.

No! this can not be happening! He should be looking at me like that. Fear tore at her. She was losing him and she didn't understand how.

In horror, Maeve watched as AJ dropped his head and pressed a soft kiss to Denise's mouth.

"Give me thirty, then we'll get out of here." He stepped away from her and hurried into Blaze's office, closing the door behind him.

Almost like a Bitch Switch flipped, Denise's cute, adoring smile transformed into one of vicious glee. She strode toward Maeve's open office door, her hips swinging, her perfect hair flowing. She was a bombshell…about to explode all over Maeve's life.

adoring **ALEJANDRO**

Fortifying herself for what was coming—or at least attempting to, she met Denise's hard, glinting blue eyes.

"Ms. Walters, what are you doing here? This isn't a White Estate office," Maeve said, her voice straining along with her smile.

Denise stopped at in front of Maeve's desk and leaned in until she was inches from Maeve's shocked face. The malicious grin on the other woman's face made Maeve's blood freeze.

"I know who you are, Maeve Thomas, office manager for Harris Construction. I know all about your little scam to get AJ to notice you." She sneered at Maeve's dropped jaw. "What? You didn't think anyone would find your emails? Figure out your plan to scheme your way into AJ's pants and pockets?" She laughed, the sound high-pitched and grating. "You're an idiot if you think your plan would have worked. You're fat, ugly, and you dress like a box troll—what makes you think he ever would have continued your little farce once he saw you in person?"

"This isn't a farce or a scheme or a scam—" Maeve just stopped herself from admitting something that would only give the love assassin more ammunition.

Too bad Denise was more perceptive than Maeve first thought.

Denise's eyes widened, her lips twisting as she stared Maeve down, fileting her skin from bone to look into her soul…and spit on it.

"Oh my God," she blurted. "You actually care about him? That's what this was all about? Some sick secret admirer thing?" She threw her head back and laughed, her tight little body vibrating with her wicked mirth.

Maeve swallowed, her mind spinning, her heart

racing—she couldn't find the words let alone the breath to speak.

This couldn't be happening! The Pennywise of White Estate IT had somehow found her emails to AJ, read them, and came up with the idea to present herself as the woman AJ had been falling for.

"Why?" The question was out before Maeve could think.

Denise cocked her head, giggling. "Why not? Everyone knows AJ is loaded. And he happens to be fucking hot. Why not take advantage of the pre-paved path to wealth and prestige?"

"You think tricking AJ will get you money and standing? The man runs a construction company. He isn't Sylvester." Sylvester, their billionaire boss, who happened to be happily in love with AJ's sister, Sally.

Denise shrugged. "He's probably one of those men who believe in working with their hands to build a legacy for their kids—blah, blah, blah. All I know is that his grandfather is a billionaire, and he has millions in the bank from an inheritance his mom left him. Loaded. Meaning that whoever gets his ring on their finger will have access to all that lovely money. And I plan for that ring, that sexy ass man, and that money to be mine."

Oh, hell no! She couldn't let her get away with that. AJ didn't deserve that!

Anger scoured her insides, turning her pain to action. She surged to her feet, leaning in to meet glare with glare. "You think I'm going to let you do that? Those are *my* emails! That was me he was falling for! That was me he met at the party—me he kissed!"

adoring ALEJANDRO

Denise quirked one eyebrow, smirking. "Oh? Did he see you? Did you two talk face to face?"

Struck dumb by the hideous truth in the bitch's words, Maeve pinched her mouth shut, the backs of her eyes burning with the need to cry until the world flooded. She leaned back, her legs wobbling. She remained standing, though. Just barely.

Denise scoffed. "I didn't think so. His last email to you indicated that you'd spent your precious time with him, fumbling around in the *dark*. It was almost too perfect. You made it all too easy for me. A poor little office mouse like you would never have the guts to show a man like AJ what you really look like. If you had, he would have run screaming—or laughed in your face. Either way, you would have ended up the sad story of the chubby wallflower who tried to bat out of her league."

Maeve drew back, squaring her shoulders. "I can tell him the truth. I don't care if he hates me or thinks I'm fat and ugly, as long as you can't manipulate him—"

Denise's diabolical grin made Maeve shudder. "It seems you forget who you're talking to, sweetie," she drawled, her words dripping with honeyed poison. "I am the director of IT. I graduated from Harvard with a cyber security degree. I can hack into your computer and make it look like you are the world's most wanted cyber terrorist, child predator, or even the plain old sex addict. I can turn your world upside down, find every connection to every person you love, then turn *their* worlds upside down. I can ruin you, your family, your friends—and even this fledgling company, all because you couldn't keep one little secret."

One little secret? Try a monumental, earth shattering secret, one that would break apart everything in her reality.

Her life torn apart or her heart shattered—those were her choices. If Denise were just threatening her, she'd deal with it. There were worse things than ending up in Guantanamo Bay or on the Megan's Law website. Her life had already been one shit thing after another, what was living the rest of her life as a hated criminal compared to what she'd already endured? But Denise had threatened Maeve's friends, too.

Anna.

Sally.

Callie.

Callie's nine-year-old daughter, Lexi.

Those beautiful, amazing women didn't deserve to have their lives—their worlds—set on fire. Lexi, especially, had already endured a life of hardship, being raised by a single mom who'd struggled through school and work to provide for her, since they'd been abandoned by Lexi's father ten years ago. Lexi deserved a happy, healthy life—something Maeve never had.

Swallowing against the urge to scream in rage and anguish, Maeve closed her eyes and nodded.

The noise that sounded like claws over glass split the air, making Maeve snap her eyes open.

Laughter. It had been evil laughter, from the evilest person.

Denise grinned, her smile cold and malicious. "You made the smart decision."

With that, she spun on her designer heels and slipped back to where AJ had left her to wait for his return.

Just as Maeve waited for the sorrow to swallow her.

adoring ALEJANDRO

An hour after "re-meeting" Denise, AJ was sitting across from her at a table on the outside patio of Kofi & Cream, a local coffee house owned and operated by Ghanaian immigrant Kofi Massi, and his Irish-American wife, Nina.

Denise waved off the coffee from the waiter, Jimmy, a kid AJ knew from summers volunteering at the youth center. "No, thanks," Denise chirped carelessly. "Can't stand the stuff. It makes me jittery, and then I can't think."

"Jimmy," AJ greeted him. "Coffee, black, and a banana nut muffin."

Denise curled her lips in distaste, but said nothing.

"And you, ma'am," Jimmy inquired politely.

Denise huffed, turning a displeased glare on Jimmy. What was her problem?

And why did he feel like getting up from the table and leaving her sitting there?

She was Swan—he should be singing from the rooftops and begging her to get the hell out of there so they could start where they'd left off on Friday night.

But he wasn't. Truth was, he was barely holding himself together, torn between wanting to ask all the questions of the woman sitting across from him and wanting to rush back to the office and beg Maeve not to hate him. She'd witnessed everything, had watched as AJ introduced Swan to Blaze, had listened as he said she was the woman he'd been waiting for his whole life. He hadn't lied, though, right? Swan was the woman behind the emails that had saved him from a life of empty one-night stands and heartache. Swan was the woman who'd made him burn and breathe again. Swan was the woman who tasted of cherry vanilla...and kissed like a seductress.

Today, though, Denise tasted of mint, and the press of her lips against his had left him cold.

Why did it feel like he'd just set fire to a stick of dynamite that would blow up his life?

Denise's sharp answer to Jimmy made AJ cringe. "I'm not a ma'am, boy. And I don't want anything unless it's dairy-free, gluten-free, and organic."

"W-we have an organic strawberry and wheatgrass smoothie, made with soy milk," Jimmy stammered, obviously uncomfortable under Denise's displeasure.

Denise thought a moment, then smiled, her face lighting up. Jimmy stood there stunned. Yeah, the woman was gorgeous, her smiles like a lifeboat for a drowning man.

But they only left *him* treading water.

"That sounds perfect," Denise said, waving a still stunned Jimmy off so he could put in their order.

Leaning back, AJ clasped his hands in his lap and stared across at Denise. In the mid-morning sun, she was beautiful. Her golden hair like a halo around her head, her bright blue eyes, beguiling in color, but striking in obvious hunger.

The thought of taking her back to his place and feeding that hunger made his cock twitch. She was the Swan he'd been fantasizing about, so his reaction was normal. Expected. She was everything a man like him could want. A walking fantasy of sensual perfection. His body demanded he reply to her blatant invitation by dragging her back to his truck and fucking her in the backseat. But his mind told him to wait. That he needed to clarify some things before he allowed his dick anywhere near her—even if she *was* Swan.

Adoring ALEJANDRO

His heart, however, was quiet. Almost…detached. As if guarding itself.

Against Swan, though? Why?

"So, tell me why," he demanded lightly. He was eager to know all, but he didn't want to push her too hard to fast. The Swan of their emails was vulnerable, skittish. She'd clam up and he wouldn't get his answers.

His gaze on Denise, he pictured her ducking her head shyly, or smiling coyly, or blushing, or…hiding behind her computer screen at all, the socially awkward, book nerd she proclaimed to be.

His thoughts turned to Maeve, as they too often did. She blushed. She smiled coyly. She tucked her chin into her chest when embarrassed. She was vulnerable, soft, gentle, but there was a fire there, a strength, a sensual spirit that blazed to life when he kissed her.

Maeve was equal parts fragile and fierce. *Stop, you're trying to make Denise—Swan—sound like Maeve.*

Denise, furrowing her manicured eyebrows at him, seemed more brittle than fragile.

"Why what?" she asked, lifting her water glass to her mouth and taking a sip. Her killer red lipstick leaving behind a deep red stain on the rim of the glass.

"Why did you send that first email? I mean, you have to know you're a beautiful woman." She visibly preened, her eyelashes fluttering. "Why did you feel like you couldn't just approach me, ask me on a real date?"

"Well, if you remember, I tried that when you were in Miami."

"True. But why not email me as yourself without all the pretense about needing to speak about business?" She'd been emailing him, texting him, and calling him regularly since they'd met in Miami several months ago. It didn't make sense that she would create a whole separate identity just to talk to him. "Why not just be upfront?"

"I was scared you'd turn me down again. And I wanted to be able to be my real self with you. I can't tell you how many men come on to me just because of my looks. I mean, yes, I'm attractive, but there's more to me than that, you know." She huffed, lifting her nose into the air with feigned indigence. The woman had no problem being ogled. Which begged the question—why had she'd been so scared to reveal herself? Why run from him Friday night when the lights came on?

Just another question to add to the growing list.

"Of course, there is more to you," he agreed. "Like mugs and baking," he offered.

"Huh?"

"There's more to you than your looks, like your mug collection, and baking cookies."

Something flashed behind her eyes.

She fumbled a laugh. "Oh. Right."

"Why do you collect mugs if you don't drink coffee?"

Her eyes widened quickly as if caught, but she quickly recovered. "Well, I make a mean mulled cider."

"Not mocha chocolate lattes? Your email said you can't go a morning without them."

She flushed, stammering, "Oh, yes, but decaf only." She smirked, her painted lips curling suggestively. "I'll have to make you some…when you come over. There's nothing like a hot cup of mocha or cider on chilly mornings."

Mornings? Because he'd come over the night before and stay until the morning?

Her words hit him…wrong. Instead of the cockstand he

should have gotten from her overt invitation to fuck, he felt nothing. His dick had lost interest in Denise once thoughts of Maeve surfaced. The woman was a cockblocker without meaning to be.

"Come over? To Miami?" he asked, something like panic suffusing his blood.

Denise slapped his arm playfully, rolling her eyes. "No, silly. My house here. I'm moving to Jackson Key. We can be together now."

That *panic* he felt moments before morphed sharply into dread as the implication of her words settled in his gut. His Swan was moving to Jackson Key, to be closer to him, so they could be together. He'd be able to kiss her, hold her, and finally make love to her. After that kiss in the dark, he was more than eager to take her mouth and then worship her body as he been longing to do for months.

So why did the thought of Denise, his Swan, wanting to take the next step in their relationship make his guts twist?

And why did the thought of Maeve seeing him with Denise make his heart ache?

chapter
THIRTEEN

AFTER A WEEK SPLIT BETWEEN WORK, SPENDING TIME with Denise, and avoiding an even quieter and more withdrawn Maeve, AJ kissed Denise goodbye. The goodbye kiss was decidedly more forced that the one he'd given her that first day—and he hated it. He hated that the woman he'd been so eager to meet no longer inspired the lust or passion she had in her emails. She'd tried to seduce him throughout the week, but he'd held her off with promises of "taking that step" after she was moved and settled, and they could continue getting to know one another. The night before her departure, she'd begged him to come with her so they could spend more time together, but he'd declined. His excuse was his it was Christmas the following week. The truth was, the thought of spending another minute with her made him jittery.

Denise was the kind of woman you handled in small doses, and one whole week with her was enough of a dose to hold him over until Armageddon.

With a pout in her lips and the promise to call and text every day, Denise headed back to Miami to start the process of listing her condo and getting her house packed for the move.

To Jackson Key. Where he lived.

The excitement he expected to feel—he *wanted* to feel—wasn't there. Instead, there was only an icy, slowly spreading anxiety.

What the fuck was wrong with him?

"Okay, what the hell is wrong with you?" Sally plopped down on the white leather couch beside him, nearly spilling the margarita in her hand. She was just on the other side of drunk, when Sassy Sallina made an appearance, and her usual filter—already dangerously thin—disappeared.

"What do you mean?" he asked, leaning forward to put his still full beer bottle on the coffee table…and to give himself something to do other than to focus on who *wasn't* there.

Maeve had been invited to spend Christmas with them, but she'd declined, telling Sally that she wasn't feeling good and wouldn't want to "intrude on a family thing" anyway.

He remembered the look on Maeve's face when she'd spotted him with Denise that first day. Pale. Stricken. So, he could guess at her sudden "illness."

God…he needed to talk to her. To explain. To apologize. He'd never meant for their—whatever the hell it was—to go as far as it did. He never meant to hurt her, though he knew he did. Maeve was a gentle soul, someone who put their whole emotions into something. And their shared kisses… they'd been passionate, hot, blazing with need, desire, and unspoken yearning. Maeve had given of herself in those kisses.

Like Swan had that night in the dark….

Shaking off that thought, AJ flicked his gaze to the open French doors. Anna was outside curled up on a lounger next to Blaze who was arguing Fantasy Football with Sly.

Though it was Christmas, it was like any other Saturday night, and AJ and his sister and their friends were settled in a Sly's beachfront mansion for a BBQ and drinks. It was a monthly tradition at that point, and one he usually looked forward to. Usually, he'd come, grab a drink, and relax after a long week of pressure and back breaking work. Usually, he could smile and laugh and actually enjoy himself. Usually, he could let his mind wonder to less important things, like what he was going to do the next morning after his morning coffee and work out. Usually, his head and heart weren't a fucking mess.

"I mean that instead of being outside with Blaze and Sly, chatting about man shit, you're in here, by yourself, brooding. You, dear brother, are a lot of things. You've never been a brooder."

He snorted, rolling his eyes. "I brood. It's part of my wicked charm. Chicks dig brooders."

Sally rolled *her* eyes, then slapped the back of his head. "You're an idiot. Chicks? Seriously? When did you descend into frat-bro-land? And don't try to get *me* to change the subject by being a douche on purpose. Tell me what has my big brother thinking so hard and looking so troubled. It is work?" Her immediate conclusion that his issues were work related made him feel like shit. Blaze and Sly were good men, they didn't deserve unnecessary shade thrown over their business, even by a well-meaning sister/girlfriend.

"Nah, nothing like that," he admitted hurriedly. "Business is good. Better than ever, actually."

She took a small sip of her drink and pinned him with a gaze she often used as a little girl, one that said, "Lay it on me, big bro."

He sighed, throwing his head back against the top of the couch, and groaning. Taking a moment, he stared at the sprigs of bright green garland and deep red berries, and white twinkle lights decorating the room. For a Florida Christmas, it was nice.

"AJ?" Sally prodded.

He heaved a sigh, his insides rolling and twisting. He knew that keeping Denise and her new role in his life a secret from his sister would bite him in the ass sooner or later. He was hoping later, though…like when he finally figured out what the hell he was supposed to do about her.

This was not how he wanted to tell his sister. Blaze and Sly knew what was going on. Sly had offered some advice in dealing with Denise: don't. Blaze still threw wary and puzzled looks his way, and had offered to listen whenever AJ wanted to talk. But both men knew better than to tell their women, who would have thrown themselves into his business without hesitation. He didn't need that kind of drama, and his best friends knew that. And he appreciated them keeping his secret, even though he got plenty of lip about in the privacy of their offices. He should have known, though, that Sally would find some way to dig up something when she wasn't even aware there was something to dig for.

"There's…this woman—"

"Holy shit! My big brother needs sisterly advice about

a woman. It's a Christmas miracle!" Sally squealed, definitely spilling her drink this time. The pink slush hitting her lap. She ignored it, placing her glass on the coffee table and snatching his hands to hold them between hers.

"Come on, AJ. Tell Sissy Sallina all about your woman problems." She sounded like Oprah, eager for celebrity dirt.

He sighed again, knowing this was going to go down in flames.

"*Women*, actually," he admitted, cringing.

Sally's mouth dropped open but shut quickly, her eyes narrowing into dangerous slits.

"I didn't take you for a cheater, Alejandro—"

He cursed, squeezing her hands hard. "No. Fuck no. It isn't like that."

She remained unmoved. "Tell me what it's like, then? Because from what you just said, you're with two women—"

"Would you let me explain before you jump to conclusions? Jesus! You're the one pushing me to open up to you, and the first thing you do is jump down my throat."

She thinned her lips, her expression changing from righteous rage to chagrined.

Sally clicked her tongue and rolled her eyes, squeezing his hands back.

"Fine. Speak. I'll listen before passing judgement."

He huffed a small laugh. "Well, thanks for that, sis."

She shrugged. "Go ahead, then."

"There's this woman…I've been speaking with her for the last almost four months. She's amazing, smart, funny, sexy, and she gives me thoughtful gifts—things she knows I like from the conversations we've had. When I think about her, I see a future—kids, the house with the fence, a happily ever after like I've always wanted. With her, I want it all, Sally."

At least until he actually met her, that was. Now...he didn't know what the hell he wanted. The memories of their conversations and then the reality of that kiss in the dark, the feelings those things elicited and what being with Denise elicited were discordant. Like two different songs playing at the same time. Like a harpsicord and a banjo, battling for musical supremacy. Neither of them coming out winners.

Her expression thoughtful, her eyes wistful, Sally offered him a smile. "She sounds wonderful, AJ. So what's the problem?"

Here we go....

"We hadn't actually met face to face. Until this week."

"But you said she's amazing and sexy and she gives you gifts.... How is that possible if you only just met her?

"It's the typical girl sends guy email, guy gets intrigued and emails girl back, and their romance is letters and couriered packages and a single kiss in a dark conference room, then a surprise visit by said woman. A TV dating show reveal, if you will."

Sally's face froze, her eyes wide as hell.

"We'll get to that kiss thing in a moment, but first...." She closed her mouth, clenching her jaw. She turned away from him, closing her eyes, and breathed deep.

Finally, after a few moments of tense silence, she opened her eyes and looked at him.

Green gemstones glittered darkly.

"Let me get this straight...you got an email from a stranger who *says* they are a woman, and you email her back. You start some sort of reckless romance via the company email server. You probably share personal, private, intimate information with this stranger…and this person sends you packages."

"Yeeesss?" he answered with a question, fearful of what she would say next. He was a grown ass man, staring down the face of his little sister, and a shame he hadn't felt before pricked at his conscience. There was no reason to be ashamed of what he had with Swan. They hadn't done anything wrong.

Why do I suddenly sound like a teenaged girl trying to explain the same thing to her dad? Because the situation was fucking ridiculous, something he refused to acknowledge.

"What, exactly, was in those packages?"

He tried to play off his mounting tension with a nonchalant shrug. "Books, movies, cookies—"

"Tell me you didn't actually eat the fucking cookies, AJ." Damn, in that moment she sounded just like a pissed off Lisana, ready to tear his ass a new one for being a little shit in her kitchen.

"I did, but I felt like I could trust her. I never, not once, felt like she was a danger to me."

She growled. "You're a romantic idiot, bro. At least you didn't die," she grumbled.

"Don't sound so put out," he teased. "Yes, I ate the cookies, and they were delicious. Ask Blaze, he's had a couple, and he didn't die, either."

She grunted and shook her head. "I will not be telling Anna that her man is eating a strange woman's cookies."

AJ snickered, glad that his sister wasn't pressing him as much as he thought she would. Then again, Sally had made a few reckless choices in her love life, including a one-night stand with a billionaire who then turned up in Jackson Key as Blaze and AJ's business partner. Thankfully, everything worked out between Sallina and Sly.

He wished he could feel the same way about his own love life.

God, he'd made a fucking mess.

"So, tell me more about this woman. You said you met her this week. What's she look like? Is she good in the sack? Wait—don't answer that last one. I don't wanna know." She shuddered.

Grinning, AJ answered, "You'll be happy to know I haven't had sex with her. We mostly spent the week chatting, getting to know one another." And discovering that spending said time with her was more like a chore than a gift.

Spending time with the Swan that showed up on Monday made him realize that…he really didn't know the woman like he thought he did.

And he told Sally just that, opening himself up to her. She was the only family he had left, and he adored her completely. Out of anyone in the world, he trusted her to give it to him straight.

After he was done spilling his guts about Swan and his week with Denise, Sally sat in silence, her gaze caught on his face, her eyes penetrating yet thoughtful.

Finally, she took his hands into hers again, and squeezed tightly.

A flash of memory…the two of them, sorrowful, grieving, standing alone and lost over the grave of their mother. In that moment, they'd only had each other. Now, their little family had grown—in number and strength. And he couldn't be more grateful to his little sister for being part of it all.

"Did you ever consider that you're just projecting what you want on to her? That you want this to be the perfect woman so badly, you're seeing perfection where there really isn't? That you're seeing something real where there is only smoke and mirrors? I mean, come on, you don't even know if this Denise woman is the one you've been talking to online. She could be an imposter. Anyone can be anyone on the internet—we've all seen the Dateline Special."

"Yeah, but the kiss at the holiday party. That was real, and it was fucking fantastic." More than. It had shaken him to his very soul, and he was still recovering. His thoughts never far from that dark room, those dark promises in her kiss, the sultry sound of her voice, the cock-hardening sounds of her moans as he took her mouth.

Fuck. Now was not the time for an erection. Not when his sister was shredding him and the mess that was his love life to pieces

"Yeah, the kiss. The one in the dark conference room. What's that about? How can you kiss someone without seeing them? Was it like two blind people bumping faces? You had to have at least touched her, right? To see if she was really…well, female. Boobs, brother. Did she have boobs?"

"One thing at a time, Sallina, shit."

She raised her hands in grudging surrender and stared at him expectantly. Practically vibrating in her seat. He was surprised Sylvester hadn't sensed a disturbance in the force and come running—as tuned into Sally's moods as he was.

"And, yes, Denise has boobs." *If it was Denise in the dark that night.* Shit! Now Sally had *him* thinking it. "I think we've talked about Swan-slash-Denise enough tonight."

"Wait," Sally blurted, "you said *women*, meaning more than one. One is the catfishing Swan, so who is the other woman?"

He *definitely* wasn't opening the Maeve can of worms

tonight. He was worn out emotionally, mentally, and physically.

"Another time, sis. Right now, I need to go home, take a long shower, and get some fucking sleep." If he could. The night ahead looked like a long one, his thoughts even more confused than ever. His heart more twisted and bleeding than ever.

Was Sally right?

Could his interest in Swan just be a figment of what he really wanted? Was he projecting onto the *silhouette* of a woman the details and emotions of what he wanted with a "real" woman?

Was he really that desperate to know love? To *give* love? Was he turning into the male version of his too trusting, too eager, too needy mother?

And what about Maeve?

He couldn't ignore the pang in his belly—and lower—when he pictured her…nor the ache in his chest when he thought of her.

Email/conference room Swan and Maeve.

How was it possible to miss two different women with the same amount of yearning? How could he desire two different women with the same level of scorching want? What kind of man did it make him that when he'd first thought of meeting Swan…he'd pictured Maeve's face?

Was he more like his lecherous, cheating father than he ever wanted to admit?

chapter
FOURTEEN

Spending the Christmas holiday alone had sucked, but it hadn't been the first time. With a family like hers—mean, selfish, and all about appearances—all holidays were beauty pageants. The only thing that changed was the theme. He dad couldn't have paid her enough to come—not that he even spoke to her anymore. It didn't hurt as much as it used to, at least.

Now, another excruciating day at work complete. Another eight hours of watching AJ, longing for AJ, and knowing she would never have him. That hurt far more than anything her dad had ever said or done. Before, when she was the pining nobody, there was still that daydream fantasy of

adoring ALEJANDRO

AJ noticing her, falling for her, and them living happily ever after. Once she'd become Swan, that daydream had turned into a full on romantic movie playing in her head and heart. AJ was falling for her, even though he didn't know her from Eve. He liked her, had begged to meet her, had admitted wanting more with her. A fat girl's dream come true.

Now, though, it was all shit.

Denise had swooped in, stolen AJ, and demolished Maeve's hopes and dreams with a single conversation. And there was nothing Maeve could do about it. She was trapped. Between choosing the *possibility* of love for herself and the happiness and safety of her friends, there was no real choice at all.

But the knowledge that her sacrifice provided safety to her friends didn't lessen the devastation.

So, she went to work, hid her agony behind a plaster smile, and tried not to give in to the urge to scream.

Thankfully, the week Denise was in Jackson Key, AJ spent most of his time out of the office. That meant Maeve hadn't had to witness him and Denise together. On the flip side, it meant that AJ was spending time with Denise outside of the office. That meant alone time. Time for more kissing…and sex.

Her heart tripped, the ache spreading into her guts, twisting them up like a hot pretzel.

No. She couldn't think about the fact that AJ had probably made love to Denise thinking *she* was his Swan. Not only did it make her sick, it made her angry! AJ was fucking an imposter. A facsimile of the one he really wanted to be with. He was sharing an intimate part of himself with someone who was using him for his money! And she couldn't say a goddamn thing!

Tossing her keys and purse on her kitchen counter, she watched as the contents of her purse spilled over the surface.

"Ugh. Just great." Lacking the energy to clean up the mess of receipts, candy wrappers, and tubes of Chapstick, she heaved a sigh. When the phone in her hand chimed, she nearly threw it against the wall. Luckily, she didn't.

Callie: That room still available?

Maeve grinned, her spirit stirring within her for the first time in over a week. Callie Williams, her best friend of best friends, was moving to Jackson Key from Nashville. She was hoping that the small town would be a better fit for her and her nine-year-old daughter, Alexstrasza. An avid World of Warcraft player in high school, Callie had been adamant about naming her only child after a character from the game. Thankfully, she allowed the nickname Lexi to be used in place of the longer, quirkier name. Which made sense, since Callie's full name was Calliope.

Callie's brother's name was Agamemnon. They called him Aggie.

Maeve: You know it is. I even bought a twin-sized air mattress for lexi to use until you can get her a bed. Its small but there's room in there for two twin beds and your clothes and things. We'll have to share the bathroom.

Callie: You are a lifesaver.

Maeve: You'd do the same for me if i needed it.

And she would. Maeve had met Callie when she was in community college in Ocala, earning her business administration degree. The met in class one day, hitting if off like fire and kindling, and since then, they'd been more like sisters than friends. After graduation, Maeve had applied for a job at White and got it. For her, the rest was history. For Callie, however, being a single mom made things more difficult. It took her a year longer than Maeve to graduate, and after she moved to Nashville to be closer to her brother, she could only find part-time work because she had to take care of Lexi, too. Unfortunately, the job she had was downsized, and she was scrambling to find something that would pay what she needed to take care of her child.

When she'd heard Callie needed help, Maeve offered what she could: a place to stay. A place where Callie and Lexi could start over.

Maeve: When should i roll out the red carpet?

Callie: Ha. Ha. We should be there thursday night, if we can get the rest of this place packed up in time. Do you still have that place for storage?

Maeve had asked Blaze if Callie could store her storage pod in the Harris Construction parking lot, and he'd said yes. The backmost part of the lot was just dirt, and no one parked there. The pod was roughly the size of a Dodge van, so it wouldn't take up too much space, and Callie could get to it easily if she needed to. And it only needed to be there until Callie could afford a place of her own.

Maeve: Yup. Everything is all set.

Callie: You don't know how much this means to us, mae. Love you!

Maeve: Can't wait to see you and the munchkin. Love you, too!

With a real smile on her face for the first time since

Denise the Destroyer strutted into town, Maeve changed into comfy clothes and threw a Marie Callender's meal in the microwave. It was a chicken, beans, and rice kind of night. Too bad she was out of tequila. She'd have to have Sally over next week, then she'd have enough booze to last her the next two months.

Meal in hand, Maeve plopped down onto her couch, grabbed the Roku remote from the coffee table, and turn on the TV. Perhaps she'd rewatch *Grimm* again. God, she loved her some Detective Nick Burkhardt. And that blut-bad wasn't too bad on the eyes, either.

A knock at the door made Maeve tense. It was seven o'clock on a Friday night. Most people she knew were out having fun, or staying in with their significant others. Suddenly wary, Maeve dropped the TV remote and headed to the door. The peephole revealed something she wasn't expecting in a hundred years.

Sliding the chain lock off, she opened the door just enough to peer at the man standing in the hallway of her apartment building.

"AJ? What are you doing here?" Dear Lord, was that her breathy, squeaky voice? She sounded like Gadget from Chip & Dale: Rescue Rangers!

Pushing past her and into her apartment, AJ stopped just behind her and waited for her to shut the door, staring at her with an unreadable emotion in his eyes.

"Uh…okay," she muttered, closing the door, and turning to him.

Her apartment was compact at only 850 square feet—since that was all she could afford. The front door opened into a tiny hallway with a coat closet on one side and the opening to the kitchen on the other. One had to walk through the kitchen to get to the small living room/dining room area. There were two bedrooms and one bathroom, but the bedrooms were small. She could just fit her queen bed and bedroom furniture. The other room, the one she was offering to Callie and Lexi, was currently a slapdash home office.

Crossing her arms over her chest, wishing she'd opted for the hoodie and not the stretched to death Book Whore sweatshirt, Maeve prodded, "Is there a reason you came here and then just invited yourself in?" She knew she sounded like a bitch, but she was goddamn entitled to be a little pissed. Life was a fucking bitch, too!

AJ rubbed his face, groaning wearily. There were dark circles under his eyes, and the laugh lines that usually creased his face were deeper. Making his face harder. His green eyes, usually twinkling with good humor were now dark. Heavy. He was tired. Worn out. And she could guess why.

It was *her* fault for starting the whole Swan thing. It was her fault AJ was confused about his feelings for Swan and whatever it was he was feeling for her. And it was her fault Denise was in his life, no doubt sucking the life force from his body like a succubus.

AJ swallowed and offered a slight smile that didn't reach his eyes. "Can we sit and talk for a minute? Blaze invited me to drinks, but I have to run home first, and, well…your place was on the way, and I just wanted to stop and say something…."

A sharp pain pierced her chest, making her breath hitch. She rubbed at the spot with a shaking hand.

He was there to tell her that things were official with Denise and he had to keep things professional between them from now on. She knew it was coming but…it still hurt like hell.

She swallowed down a pained sob and forced a smile. "Sure. Come in." She led him through the kitchen and into the living room. She waited for him to take a seat on the loveseat and she took a seat in the small wicker chair with the handmade cushions with the palm trees on it. It was meant to be patio furniture, but it was also a cheap seating option in a small living space.

Seated, she clasped her hands in her lap, forced her gaze to his face, and held her breath.

He rubbed his face again, looking world worn and anxious.

"AJ?" She was well aware that she sounded raspy. Anguished. How could she not? She was grieving a loss of something she'd wanted her whole life. And it was sitting just there…but still out of reach.

"I shouldn't have kissed you," he blurted, making Maeve flinch. He met her gaze, regret burning in his green eyes. "I never should have allowed this to go beyond a professional relationship."

Words failing her, she said nothing.

"I know you're friends with Sally and Anna, so we'll have to be friendly with one another. But…do you think that you can do that, be my friend as well as my office manager, without it getting weird?"

Oh…it was so much *weirder* than that already.

Another forced smile. "Of course. No worries, AJ. We're both adults, we can keep things as friendly or professional as you want."

He stared at her, his expression closed, his lips thinned as though holding back.

Finally, he nodded, offering a sad smile of his own. "Okay. Good."

He stood and she shot to her feet.

What? That was it? That was all he came to say? That couldn't be it, there had to be more!

Suddenly desperate for him to stay, she reached out and snagged his bare forearm, the contact sending electricity zapping through her. She gasped at the sensation.

"Is this about Denise?" she bleated, her pride taking a hit at the neediness in her voice.

AJ furrowed his brow, his sad smile turning into a frown. He looked down at her hand on his arm and she dropped it like it was on fire. Her fingers curled—that simple, innocent touch of his flesh making her nerve endings tingle.

His frown deepened.

Why the frown? Shouldn't him finally being with Denise, *his Swan*, make him happy?

Shouldn't my misery mean his *happiness?* She could hear the sneer of her inner thoughts.

She wanted to scream!

"Denise and I are doing great," he replied, his tone forced. "Honestly, I can't *believe* she's the woman I've been talking to all these months. It all seems…surreal."

"What do you mean you can't believe it's her?" Maeve's heart rate galloped.

He opened his mouth to reply then seemed to think better of what he was going to say.

The smile he offered was lopsided, more like the AJ she'd fallen in love with. Her racing heart veered right off the track. Yeah, there was no way he was unhappy with bombshell Denise Walters. The woman was walking sex and sin, and AJ was walking orgasms and bliss. Denise was tall, blonde, stacked, and a bitch. AJ was tall, hard, gorgeous, and so, so sweet. Physically, they were the perfect match of beauty and build. Their hearts, though…. But maybe AJ didn't care about the heart. He'd taken one look at Denise and believed her bullshit about being Swan. Even after all the pieces of her heart and soul that Maeve had shared via email, AJ was too blinded by perky tits and pouty lips to realize that Denise couldn't possibly be Swan.

Don't blame him for this! This is all your fault. You should have just grown a pair of lady balls and told him the truth from the beginning.

No. She couldn't be angry at AJ for choosing Denise over the shadow of an outline of an idea of feelings he *might* have for Maeve.

But there was nothing Maeve could say or do without hurting everyone she cared about.

And if you say nothing, the man you love will end up married to a greedy harpy.

Lose-lose. No matter what she died, she was lost.

AJ's humorless chuckle wrung Maeve from the tumble of her thoughts.

"I mean that I can't believe she's actually real, and that I can finally be with her," he remarked. "Yeah. Totally unreal, ya know?"

Yes. Unreal. Unbelievable. Unfathomable.

Striding by the kitchen peninsula, AJ glanced down then seemed to freeze in place. As she watched, he turned toward the counter, peering down at the crap from her purse. What? Did she forget there was a tampon in there?

He reached out and picked up one of the five tubes of Chapstick from the clutter.

Lifting it to his face, he sniffed it.

adoring **ALEJANDRO**

Uh…what?

"What are you doing?" she asked, truly and utterly puzzled about his fascination with her lip balm.

Without turning to her, his voice low and flat, he murmured, "Cherry."

Huh?

"Yeah. I think that one's the Cherry Vanilla Coke one Callie sent me as a stocking stuffer last Christmas. She sent me a whole pack of them." She cocked her head, suddenly anxious. "Why?"

"Do you…do you wear it often?" What was with the questions about her lip moisturizer?

"Uh…yeah. It's my favorite. Is there a reason you're so curious about my choice of Chapstick?"

"You don't wear it at the office," he observed.

"With all the coffee I drink, I don't bother. I just comes off on the cup."

"Coffee…" he muttered, his body stiff. She tensed in response, unsure where this was all going.

"Uh…I use those mocha chocolate coffee packs from Swiss Miss." His body jerked as if she'd hit him.

"Why?" she asked, suddenly wary.

Instead of answering her question, he simply put the Chapstick back on the counter, shook his head, and continued on his way out of her apartment.

No other words were exchanged.

Not even goodbye.

Flummoxed, Maeve stared at the closed door for long minutes, trying to wrap her head around AJ's visit, his questions, and that thing about her Chapstick.

Was there something wrong with cherries?

You taste like cherries….

Everything within her froze in place.

Oh.

Oh no.

She'd worn that Chapstick the night of the holiday party when she'd kissed him in that dark conference room. He'd even commented on it in his email.

And the weirdness about the coffee?

God. Oh shit. She'd told him about her mocha coffee obsession in her Swan emails. Was he starting to put the pieces together? Was that why he'd come by to talk to her, even though their conversation was aborted before it even really began?

She'd figured he was there to tell her that whatever was between them was over now that Denise was in the picture, but...he didn't seem as convinced.

Does that mean I have a chance? Did that mean he wasn't as easy to fool as Denise believed he was. Certainly, the man wasn't idiot. He could figure things out if he felt even an inkling of suspicion. Denise must have done something to make AJ question her insistence that she was his Swan. Suddenly, her early snide thoughts about AJ being fooled by perky tits made her cringe.

Good! That means we still have a chance!

No! No, it didn't. Denise was still the enemy, still holding Maeve hostage with her cyber terror threats. There was nothing Maeve could do but watch silently, and hope AJ dropped Denise before things got too serious—before Denise got her claws in his heart and his wallet.

Before AJ really got hurt.

And before Maeve truly lost him forever.

chapter FIFTEEN

Finally, after waiting all fucking day, AJ was ready to relax with a cold beer and his friends. Rather than the usual meet and eat at Happy Jack's, Sally and Anna wanted to mix it up by having everyone out to Tony's. With the best pizza and most laid back atmosphere in town, Tony's was the perfect place to just eat and chill. There was also room to spread out, since Sally mentioned that Maeve's friend from college was coming into town that night.

Just then, a tiny dervish sped past, making Blaze and AJ jump out of the way. The speed demon slammed into Maeve, making the woman stumble back. In a flash, AJ was there, throwing his arm out behind her, catching her before she could fall on her ass. Her lush, bitable ass.

Huffing, her face turning that delicious pink, Maeve ducked her head and muttered a quick thanks before moving away, taking her lush curves and sensuous body heat with her.

His arms felt empty. They ached for her to return to them. To wrap around her. Hold her.

He couldn't ignore the fact that he didn't feel the same for Denise.

God, he was fucked up.

"Lexi!" Maeve called, throwing her arms out, her face lighting up. Her smile, which had always seemed to hide when he was around lately, shone like the sun filling the sky after a hurricane.

"Auntie Maeve!" the little blonde girl squealed, rushing to launch herself into Maeve's open arms. Maeve caught her, tightening her arms around the child, burying her face in the girl's neck, and squeezing.

"Lexi Love! It is so good to see you, baby girl!"

The girl giggled, leaning back to grin at Maeve. "Do it!"

Maeve's brow wrinkled in confusion. "Do what?"

Little Lexi giggled and rolled her wide blue eyes. "The voice, silly! I want to hear the princess voice!"

Maeve chuckled then nodded. "You got it, Queen Lexi!" While the little girl waited, her expression expectant, Maeve did something that made AJ's eyes snap to her.

"Oh, my *dahling*, I am so happy to see you again! I do so hope the palace is to your liking and that you will enjoy your time here."

AJ blinking, her brow furrowing. *What*....

Something wasn't....

Was it something she'd said that slammed against his brain like a bullet in a cast iron barrel?

No.

"You aren't supposed to speak...."

The *voice*. The one Denise had explained away as a way to continue the mystery.

Funny how whenever he brought it up, she always changed the subject or told him she didn't perform on command or that she didn't feel in the mood to playact.

But the woman in the room that night...her voice had been smooth. Confident. Like she was an actual Briton sliding into the shadows of a White Estate conference room.

"Yes, please kiss me...."

He breath caught, burning in his lungs as he fought to exhale.

"Princess Maeve!" Lexi chirped, laughing.

"Queen Lexi! I must say, you look absolutely beautiful today. Who did your hair?" She flipped the girl's hair playfully, then tugged on the girl's flouncy, floral top. "What are you wearing?"

Everything stopped.

"What are you wearing?"

It was *her* voice. That same accent, too. She—*Swan*—had asked that *same* question of him that night that he'd first tasted her. First heard her groans of pleasure. First heard her speak his name.

The voice from the shadowed conference room.

From the holiday party.

From the night his whole life changed.

Wait...what? But it hadn't been *Maeve* that night—it had been Denise. *She* was the one who'd approached him that

Monday after, revealing the truth. It had been Denise who had given him all the printed emails as proof it had been her.

Emails can be forged.

No, not those emails. They were identical to the ones he'd sent Swan. *His* Swan. It was Denise. She knew all the things he'd only shared with Swan.

She probably read the emails. Even then, though, when he'd brought up things Swan had spoken about in her emails—mugs, baking, and even her love of off-beat supernatural TV shows—Denise had seemed to trip over her responses, like she was coming up with the answers on the spot, rather than already having the truth at hand.

And it wasn't just that that felt off about her. In her emails she seemed thoughtful, kind, like she went out of her way to do for others. The Swan who manifested as Denise had been rude, thoughtless, and pushy. The Swan of the emails was self-deprecating, and was shy about herself. She'd hidden in the dark for their first kiss, for God's sake. The Swan that rode into town in the BMW was well aware of her charms, and had tried to use them at every opportunity.

The accent, the personality shift, the wrongness.

Things didn't add up, but what other conclusion could he come to when the real Swan hadn't put a stop to the supposed Swan imposter? Also, the emails from Swan had stopped. That could mean that she'd revealed herself as Denise and didn't need to continue the charade…or that the "real" Swan disappeared completely, never having really existed at all.

So, was Denise really Swan? His gut was telling him no…and that only made him more frustrated. Angrier. All he wanted was to love and be loved. How the hell had it all gotten so twisted and complicated. He just wished he could make sense of everything. He just wanted the Swan from the emails to be real, and be…someone other than Denise.

He sighed, pressing the bridge of his nose between his fingers. Stress headaches had become a thing for him. He was popping Advil like they were candy, and he spent more time tossing in turning in bed than he did actually sleeping.

Instead of falling to sleep after a backbreaking day at the job site, he was ruminating on thoughts and questions that would probably never have answers.

Where would Denise have gotten the emails if she wasn't the one he'd been emailing?

Then, the answer hit him so hard and fast, he nearly fell to his knees.

Denise Walters. *Director of IT*. She'd have access to *all* email accounts connected to the White Estate Corporation servers.

Like the accounts used by Harris Construction employees.

Like him.

And—fuck, he couldn't believe he was about to consider this….

Like *Maeve*.

Just thinking her name unlocked his thoughts as things started to align in his mind. Like blue sky appearing through black storm clouds.

Lexi's excited squeal broke AJ from his spiraling, frantic, revealing thoughts.

If the woman in the conference room was Maeve, why hadn't she said anything when Denise showed up claiming it was her? Why hadn't she come forward, disproving Denise's claims that she was Swan? She'd had weeks already to tell the truth, and she could have revealed herself months ago. It wasn't like he'd been an ogre to her at the office.

Yeah, but you weren't really a prince, either. He'd largely ignored her, been all business with her. He hadn't even had a personal conversation with the woman until that morning with the cookies situation. If she was Swan, of course she'd hide behind a computer screen—the office side of the screen wasn't all that great.

There was so much more to this than he was prepared to think about right then, especially since Maeve's blue gaze was pinned to him, concern etched into her lovely features.

And they were lovely. So lovely.

How had he not noticed that before?

Because you never looked at her like "that". With an appreciative male eye. Not until that night at Velvet, when you acted like a total ass to her.

Ugh. And he was still walking on eggshells around her for that. There wasn't anything he could say that would bring back the smile she'd worn that night, when she'd been so open, carefree, brilliant, and fearless. Nothing he could do to get her to let her walls down around him like they had been that night, when she was more alive and alight than she ever was at the office.

At least she wasn't wearing brown anymore.

And that was one of the problems he'd been having lately. Since that night at the club, it was almost as if Maeve had been body snatched and switched with a more confident, carefree, sensual Maeve—at least in fashion. Sally had made Maeve her living doll, dressing her in clothes that did nothing to hide her luscious femininity from hungry male eyes. She'd become a Maeve he appreciated way too much for his liking.

But if she really is Swan, it would make sense. His inability

adoring **ALEJANDRO**

to focus with her around, the draw he felt toward her even when she wasn't around. The need to see her, talk to her… just be with her.

If she was Swan, she had a lot of fucking explaining to do. And so did Denise.

"Alexstrasza Marie Williams!" A woman with frizzy red curls, and a flushed face, dressed in tight jeans, loose t-shirt, and cowboy boots blasted into Tony's family seating room, glaring at the little girl. "You about gave me a heart attack! You can't go running off like that!"

The little girl tucked her wobbling chin into her chest and pouted. "But Mama, I was just coming to see Auntie Maeve. I missed her so, so much."

Oh hell…that little girl was trouble with an adorable T.

"Tell you what, munchkin," Maeve cooed, dropping her posh accent. "Once you and your momma are settled, you and I will bake a batch of chocolate-chocolate muffins. How does that sound?"

The little girl squealed, jumping up and down. Her mother grinned down at the girl, then at Maeve.

"Auntie Maeve, always baking up something delicious. Lord, I missed your baking, woman."

Baking.

Maeve *did* bake, didn't she?

Voices, conversations, and the sounds of the restaurant muffled as if through water. Unbidden, his thoughts narrowed to a pinpoint, laser focused on one person.

Maeve Thomas.

What did he know about Maeve? She was efficient, hardworking, intelligent, and she was a good friend to his sister and Anna.

But what *else* did he know about her? Over the course

of the last month alone, he'd learned more than he had in the months she'd already worked for Harris.

Mentally, he jotted down a list.

She baked. Swan baked delicious cookies.

She could fake a brilliant British accent. Swan spoke with the same accent.

She had an out of control mug collection. Swan had an out of control mug collection.

She loved mocha chocolate coffee. Swan obsessed over the stuff.

She knew were AJ lived. Swan had couriered her care packages right to his doorstep.

She worked at White before taking the position at Harris. Swan had been at the company party, and knew details about the building a visitor wouldn't.

Maeve used Cherry Vanilla Coke Chapstick. Swan tasted of cherries and vanilla.

He might not have spent a lot of time with Maeve outside of the office, but from what he did know of her, how she was with Sally and Anna, and how she was with clients, Blaze, Sly, and even him, she was a sweet, thoughtful, funny, and quick witted woman—if a little socially awkward. What he knew of Swan from her emails told him that, in person, she was everything Maeve was…but also sexy. Maeve was gorgeous. Sensual. A woman of passion wrapped tightly in uncertainty and shyness. She had no idea of her appeal, as though she'd been hiding too long. Behind beige and boxy clothes. In the office, she was a mouse. That night at Velvet, she'd been a vixen.

Maeve was like two different women, both of them intriguing.

Both of them tying him up in knots.

Was it possible? Could Maeve be Swan?

If so, what the fuck did Denise have to do with it? Were they working together to make a fool of him?

He immediately discounted that.

Maeve—in either iteration—wasn't that kind of woman. If she was, Sally and Sly would have sniffed her out long before now. AJ trusted those two and their bullshit meters with his life and career. If they'd, for a moment, thought that Maeve was something other than what she portrayed, she never would have made it into their inner circle. But, there she was, chatting with his friends and family as if she belonged.

She does belong.
With you.
Dammit.

Pulling his cell from his pocket, he couldn't stop himself from taking a leap from the ledge without the promise of solid ground to land on.

AJ: You look beautiful tonight.

He heard the text ping through to Maeve's phone, a smile he didn't even bother fighting curling his lips. If he was right about his assumptions, his night just got a whole lot better.

Maeve held up her hand to her friend, pulled her cell from her pocket, and peered down at it. He nearly groaned in delicious pleasure when her cheeks turned pink. Was that the same pink she turned all over when she was aroused?

He was determined to find out.

If Maeve *was* Swan, she was meant to be his. They'd deal with the consequences later.

After he seduced the truth from her cherry vanilla lips.

chapter
SIXTEEN

MAEVE STARED DOWN AT THE TEXT AND NEARLY FELL to the floor in shock.

AJ: You look beautiful tonight.

Uh. What the hell? Before she could respond, Callie bumped her shoulder.

"What's got you looking like you just saw one of those kissing movies you always denied watching?"

Maeve laughed, bumping Callie's shoulder right back.

Throwing her arms around her friend, she squeezed tight.

"God, I missed you. I am so glad you and Lexi decided

to move here. I was beginning to think I wouldn't see you again until Lexi was a grandmother."

Callie snorted. "That girl already acts old enough, let's not rush things, 'kay?"

Giggling, Maeve hugged her friend again. It was so good to have Callie there. She hadn't realized how much she needed her friend until she saw her and Lexi again. It was like an ache she didn't know she had—because she'd gotten used to it—had finally lifted. It wasn't as though Sally and Anna weren't good friends, good people, it was that Maeve and Callie had been through a lot together. Callie knew more about Maeve than anyone else.

And you can unload all your shit about AJ on her and she won't think you're crazy.

But she couldn't tell Callie. Because Callie would rage, race her ass to Miami, and snatch the hair off Denise's head—and Denise would realize that Maeve hadn't kept her end of the bargain.

No. Maeve couldn't tell Callie.

After a few more moments of chit chat and spontaneous hugs, Anna and Sally sidled up to Maeve and Callie for introductions. Thankfully, the women seemed to get along perfectly—like Callie was a missing component to their group.

"So, Maeve says you're looking for work." Anna was all business all of a sudden, which wasn't a surprise. Anna was always looking for opportunities to help.

Callie nodded. "Sure am. With the kiddo I only have time for part-time work, so in Nashville the pickin's were slim."

"You have a business admin degree?" Sally asked, sipping her glass of water.

"Yup. Sadly, most places hiring for business

administration want full-time. I can only work with Lexi is in school. Ultimately, I'd like to open my own business, but I need a steady job first. Banks need proof of income before they'll just hand you money."

Anna tapped her chin in thought. "You have any waitressing experience?"

Callie gave a quick nod and grinned, her cognac-colored eyes filling with hope. "I sure do. You got something for me?"

Chuckling at Callie's enthusiasm, Anna replied, "Greg at Happy Jack's is looking for a waitress for the afternoon shift. The afternoons are slower and the tips aren't all the great, but the work is steady. You'd be working with me." With a brilliant smile, Anna threw an arm over Callie's shoulder. "That should be incentive enough to apply for the job."

The group laughed.

"I'll come by tomorrow to apply, how does that sound?" Callie said, her lips quirking.

"Sounds like we're going to be work besties."

Maeve couldn't stop the warm, joyful smile. She was relieved that her best friend had been so warmly embraced by her new friends. Not that Sally and Anna would be anything but wonderful and welcoming.

"Mama, can I have a soda?" Lexi peered up at her mom, her long black lashes fluttering in a well-practiced manner. The placemat before her was covered in crayon markings and tic-tac-toe using crayons provided by the hostess.

Callie snorted. "You can fan those things at me all you like, missy, but it's too close to bedtime for sweets."

Lexi huffed, crossing her little arms over her chest to pout.

Seated at the twelve-seater table, they dug in once the pizza and breadsticks arrived. Maeve, seated between Callie and Lexi, allowed herself to be taken away by the closeness and conversation of her long-time friend and her daughter. It felt good to have them there. It felt like, after too many wrongs, something was going right.

Distracted by what was going on around her, Maeve had nearly forgotten about the text she'd received right before it all started.

Flicking her gaze to the man across the table chatting with Blaze and Sly, she nearly melted in a pool of need when his gaze landed on her. Green fire. He smirked, driving the need deeper. She sucked in a breath and, with a trembling hand, took her phone from her pocket. Spying the beer on the table by his plate, she texted him.

Maeve: Are you drunk?

Lord, what else could she ask? The man was obviously inebriated. No one who was sober would taunt her with a text like that, and then send her "fuck me" eyes and a wicked smile. Maeve barely noticed when Callie stood to take Lexi to the bathroom, leaving the seats on either side of her empty.

AJ's phone pinged and his smirk grew into a full-blown grin, one that made her blink at the blinding-ness of it. Holey sheet.

AJ: Sober as a priest, but definitely not as sanctified.

Maeve: We're all sinners.

She attempted to keep her response light, even though she knew AJ was going for naughty. But why?

AJ: You're right, and i'm feeling awfully sinful right now.

Her core clenched hotly, her nipples hardening. Ah hell.

How was it possible for words to have such an effect on her? Oh yeah. It was AJ. The man owned her, body and soul.

But he was with Denise. So what was with the flirtatiousness and the filthy looks?

Maeve: i don't even know what to say. What is going on with you?

Sly's booming laughter filled the room, joined by something Blaze said, startling her. She nearly dropped her phone but caught it just as Sally slid into Callie's empty seat beside her. Sally's gaze flit between Maeve and AJ, a knowing smile spreading across her face like the Cheshire Cat.

"You and my brother, huh?"

Maeve coughed, pounding a fist against her chest, desperate to think up *werds* in response. Sally couldn't know what was going on. If she figured things out, things would get way more complicated than they already were. Sally, ever perceptive, knew something was up, and she was digging as only a friend and sister would. Her intentions were good, but her methods were diabolical.

"He's a good boss," Maeve replied, tucking her phone and the flaming red flag of texts back into her pocket.

Sally wiggled her eyebrows. "Boss? Is that what you call him when you're alone?"

"I call him AJ all the time, and we're rarely alone. We work in an office, Sally." *That's right. Keep your responses flat and unemotional. She won't figure anything out from the blush on your cheeks or the way you can't stop looking over at AJ who is not helping.* The man was staring at her, his arms crossed, like he was waiting for her to break into song and dance. Anyone looking at them would think something was up, but there was nothing *to be* up between them. He'd seen to that with his apology and insistence they be work friends.

Work friends didn't send flirty texts, though. Something was up with him, and Maeve didn't have the mental energy nor emotional fortitude to deal with it. She wanted to finish the night, take Callie and Lexi home, and settle in.

Sally struck a nonchalant pose, one arm crossed over her chest, one elbow planted on the crossed arm, and a manicured fingernail tapping on her chin.

"You know…my brother told me something last Friday that I just couldn't believe…."

Don't show interest. Sally would pick apart any facial expression.

"Oh?" *That's good. Nice and simple.*

Sally continued, "He told me he was finally settling down, and that he'd met this woman—get this—through a secret admirer email. Can you believe it? Supposedly this woman is so great and wonderful, he's moving her to Jackson Key."

Stunned, Maeve couldn't hold the mask of indifference in place. She dropped it, and her heart followed suit. She sucked in a breath, her body losing all heat.

No. No! Things were moving too fast. Denise couldn't possibly have won already.

It's not like she had any opposition! You're letting her get away with murder!

"O-oh. That's good for them. She seemed…nice." *Nice and fucking horrible!*

Sally leaned back in the seat and pinned Maeve with a speculative look. Before she could open her mouth to continue her well-intentioned mind fuckery, AJ's voice broke between them.

"Sally, leave Maeve alone. Whatever you just said to her made her white as a sheet."

Sally pursed her lips and scowled at him before her expression changed to concern. "I didn't mean to do that."

"It doesn't matter what you meant to do," AJ growled, rising to his feet to hurry around the table to Maeve's side. "Come on, Maeve. You look like you could use some air." Her mind trapped in a whirlpool dragging her down to drown her, she didn't fight AJ as he pulled her to her feet and led her out the restaurant doors, around the corner, and to a red brick wall. He leaned her against it.

"Breathe, Maeve," he commanded.

She sucked in a breath and pinched her eyes shut. She would not cry. She would not cry. She'd brought this on herself. On AJ. Denise had won. She had lost. Everything. But she would not cry.

But anger was fucking warranted. Her hands trembling, her body began to shake off the shock as red hot anger surged through her. Anger at herself, her circumstances, and fucking Denise! Anger at life and how it obviously hated her. Anger at AJ for being so goddamn wonderful and beautiful that she'd fallen for him in the first place.

"What the hell happened back there? What did Sally say that made you look like you were going to die on the spot?"

Pushing away from the wall, Maeve began to pace. Her arms swinging madly, her shoulders pulled in to keep her temper in check. Her mind screamed, unhinged. She was breaking apart.

"What the fuck, Maeve—talk to me," AJ demanded, reaching out to grab her arm and stop her mad pacing.

Crack. She broke.

She glared at him, snatching her arm from his grasp.

He recoiled, his eyes wide, his mouth dropping open. So, he wasn't expecting the pissed off Maeve. Well, she was done being the mouse, it was time to be the lioness.

She spun on her heel, lifted her chin, squared her shoulders, and pinned him with a eyes filled with every atom of hurt and rage.

AJ remained rooted to the spot, his eyes narrowing at her, his hands fisting at his sides, as if bracing for impact.

Boom, motherfucker!

"Is Denise moving to Jackson Key?" she inquired sharply, not caring that she sounded like a bitch. She *was* a bitch. Circumstances required it.

AJ grit his teeth, his eyes twitching.

Oh, so *he* was angry now. Goodie.

"Is that what that was about in there? Sally told you that Denise was moving here and you got, what? Mad?" he seethed. "You don't get to be mad about that, *Maeve*."

She didn't miss how he emphasized her name. What that meant, she had no idea.

She planted her hands on her hips, and growled, "I'm not mad, AJ. Fuck you. Because I'm not allowed to be mad, right? I'm not allowed to care that the biggest bitch in all of Florida is slithering into my town, and touching my—"

She snapped her mouth shut, her chest heaving with shaking breaths. God—she'd almost spilled everything.

Snarling, she gripped her forehead with both hands and spun away from AJ, determined to put several feet and maybe several miles between them. She couldn't do it. No matter how frustrated and disappointed and hurt she felt, she couldn't' sacrifice her friends. Letting anything slip now… AJ would pick at it until he started to figure things out. And then Denise would be unleashed upon her.

EVE BLACK

AJ's hand reached out, grabbing her arm and flinging her against the brick wall. She hit it with an *oomph* before he was there, pinning her in place with one hand on each side of her head. His forearms flexed as he leaned in, his nose an inch from hers.

"Finish it, Maeve. Finish what you were saying," he urged, his tone as hard as the chest pressed against her and the wall behind her. "Denise is coming into your town and touching your…*what?*" He leaned in closer, brushing his nose against her cheek. She shuddered, the heat of him, the nearness, the scent of him, it caressed her as no hand ever could. "Tell me, *Maeve*. What of yours is Denise touching?"

What did he want her to say? *He'd* been the one to break off any chance of something between them. He'd been the one to come to her home and tell her they could only be friends.

"Move," she commanded. "I need to get back inside to Callie." Squeezing her hands in between them to press against his chest. Lord, he was so hard. So hot to the touch. She'd give anything to know what his naked chest felt like beneath her hands.

He didn't move. She braved looking up into his face, and immediately wished she hadn't. Fire wrought of fury and desire. Lust and indignation. He was a writhing, vibrating mass of need and frustration—and he was aimed right at her.

She shivered, her body quaking in answering need and rage.

"You're hiding again. Mouse. Where did the woman from *Velvet* go, huh? Where did the woman of just a minute ago run off to? What is it that you are hiding? *Who* are you hiding from, *Maeve?*"

She pushed at his chest again. Again, he didn't move.

"Are you hiding from this?"

He took her mouth, violating her lips in a kiss so hard and aggressive, she couldn't catch her breath—and she didn't care. Like two animals devouring one another, their kiss turned hotter, harder, more punishing. Reaching down, AJ grabbed Maeve's thigh, dragging it up until she was forced to wrap her leg around him, her foot lodged firmly against his rock-hard ass.

Breaking the kiss, he growled, "Fuck!"

Dizzy from the lack of oxygen, she couldn't only agree.

Grinding his erect cock into her belly, he growled. "You feel that? That is me, wanting you."

She whimpered.

"I know you're wet, that your pussy is aching, soaking wet. If I put my hands between your legs, will they come out sticky and covered in your cream. If I put those fingers in my mouth, will I taste your arousal? Would it taste like cherry vanilla?"

She shook her head, hot desperate lust pulsing through her.

"N-no, it isn't like that," she stuttered.

His lips curled, and she didn't know whether to slap his face or attack it with her mouth.

"No?" he drawled huskily. "Let's find out, shall we?"

No! This is wrong. He belongs to Denise!

With one mighty shove at his chest, AJ stumbled backward, the back of his hand pressed to his mouth, though it couldn't hide the filthy smirk that curled his kss-swollen lips.

"Fuck you," Maeve whimpered, running toward the restaurant doors as fast as her weakened legs could carry her.

Dark, wicked laughter following after.

EVE BLACK

From the Desk of AJ Mendez

January 14th

I miss you. I can't wait to see you again, my Swan. I can't wait to kiss you again. I can't wait to hold you in my arms once more. I know it probably makes me sound like I'm pussy whipped, but I don't give a shit. I am in this. Full stop. I want it all with you, baby. The house. The wedding. The kids. The future.

When I see you again, there's something I want to give you.

I promise you'll like it.

Forever yours,
AJ

chapter
SEVENTEEN

AFTER PULLING HIS TRUCK INTO HIS SPOT AT HARRIS Construction, AJ was greeted by a text that made his stomach curl in on itself. He cursed.

Denise: I can't wait to see you, either, baby. I can be there this weekend. Can i have a hint about my gift?

"Shit," he hissed, dragging himself from his truck and toward the office doors.

He'd known that using the Swan email account was probably a bad idea, but he wanted to continue the charade with "Swan" just a little bit longer. *Of course*, Denise got the email, too—she'd gotten her hands on the other ones. How, though? It wasn't like Maeve handed them to her and then gave a by your leave for Denise to pursue a romance with AJ using Maeve's words. If he had one guess, he guessed Denise got access to the Swan emails through her position as the IT director. But how had she known those first emails at all? Why had she even been looking in his private emails in the first place?

The woman has been after your cock for weeks now. Would she take the pursuit too far, digging into his work emails to spy on him? Yes, after that first email from Swan he should have had her email him at her personal email address, but he'd been scared that she would balk at changing things up. Over the months, though, he should have taken that step. Now, Denise had emails that basically detailed his personal hopes, dreams, and sexual fantasies, things he'd only meant for Swan to know.

The invasion of privacy was catastrophic. Thankfully, he hadn't shared anything that would be considered taboo or would lead to reputation killing situations if the information got out. Sure, he'd get some sideways glances from clients, but it wouldn't hurt. Too much.

Denise's invasion of his private life was a serious issue, one he needed to figure out before things with Maeve got more serious.

Maybe he could talk to Maeve and ask her about it.

He rolled his eyes at that.

No. As angry as Maeve was at Tony's, she'd bolt the second AJ spoke Denise's name. It was bad enough that Maeve had born witness to AJ's actions and words the morning Denise had falsely pronounced herself the Swan from the emails.

Uh huh, like you weren't a little bit convinced Denise was telling the truth.

Fuck. Yes. He could admit to himself that after his initial reservations about Denise, he'd wanted to believe she really was Swan. She was gorgeous, polished, and his body had responded to her. But once he'd actually sat down with her, had a conversation with her, everything felt off. That first rush of attraction fell away, leaving only a numbness.

Something he'd never experienced with Maeve. Even when she was hiding as the office mouse, he'd been aware of her, his gaze always going to her, his thoughts catching on her in the quiet moments. She might have believed no one noticed her unless they needed something from her, but from the second she stepped into the office, AJ had seen her. He'd noticed.

He just hadn't noticed that he'd…noticed. Until she'd emerged from her shell at Velvet and struck him hard and fast. He'd been blindsided by his attraction for her, having believed his focus on her had been harmless. Professional.

Bullshit.

With her, his body and mind were drawn to her. Her quiet sensuality, her rare smiles the could power an ecosystem, her understated wit, and her warmth and thoughtfulness. Everything he'd learned about Maeve, everything he'd seen of her with him and others, it all drew him in. It was like an unintentional seduction, one that teased all of him at once.

Denise was a practiced seductress, while Maeve had no idea the power of her charms.

Striding into the office, he couldn't stop himself from looking for Maeve. Her office door was shut. He stopped, staring at it. That door was rarely shut that early in the morning, since Maeve was in and out making the coffee, running the copy machine, and getting the office tidied up for clients.

The fact that her door was shut meant she was once again hiding.

From him.

That kiss the night before had turned him inside out and thrown him on his head. Never in his life had a kiss ignited him as that one had. He was willing to admit that he'd had more than his fair share of kisses. He was red-blooded, surging with the sexual passions of his Latin ancestors. He loved to fuck. Was extremely good at it. He could kiss, could make any woman drop her panties with a single press of his mouth to hers. Not once had a kiss ever made him want to strip a woman bare and sink inside her on the spot. Until last night. Maeve's mouth was heaven, hot and fucking delicious. He could have kissed her forever, but the drive to take her, to claim her, make her his had been so strong, he would have fucked her against the side of the building without any care about who was watching.

Maeve's kiss made him lose his goddamn mind. And he wanted to do it again and again and again. Forever. The rest of his life.

Maeve's kisses were his.

So what was he going to do about it now that his suspicions about Denise had come to fruition? Now that he knew Maeve was Swan, he had two options.

He could confront her.

He could wash his hands of her.

The latter wasn't even an option at all. He couldn't do without Maeve. She was quickly becoming his everything—and it was driving him crazy to not know what the hell to do about the situation in which he'd found himself.

First, he knew he had to drop Denise and cut all ties with her. That woman was a grasping harpy, a liar, a schemer.

adoring ALEJANDRO

No doubt she'd probably heard about his money and was angling to get her hands on it. Really, he should have her brought up on charges of impersonating with the intent to defraud. That was a mess. He'd rather just leave her deceitful ass in Miami and have Sly fire her.

Next, he needed to get Maeve to admit she was Swan. That would be tricky, however, since the woman currently believed he and Denise—the imposter Swan—were a couple. But he couldn't let the potential consequences stop him from trying to get the woman of his dreams to finally reveal herself to him.

He had to get her some place where she couldn't run, but it would take some cunning. And probably some help from Blaze.

Grinning as a plan formed in his mind, he threw his stuff on his desk and took another long look at Maeve's closed office door.

She was hiding now, but last night she'd been like fire in his arms. She wanted him as much as he wanted her, and he could work with that.

It was time for him to man the fuck up and get his woman.

I'll let you hide for now, Maeve, but I will make you mine.

And, fuck, he couldn't wait to have her mouth against his again, her body writhing in his arms. Her taste on his tongue. Her moans of pleasure in his ears. And finally, he would have her beneath him, wrapped around him.

He would claim her, and she would claim him right back.

Their beginning wasn't normal—it was ludicrous, really. But what they'd created after that first email was something that he would always cherish. Because it had awoken something inside him that had been asleep in the dark and damp, bringing it to life in the light and heat. All the years before, he'd been going through the motions, fucking and taking, and feeling nothing. One letter from Swan—from Maeve—and it was like he was reborn. Remade. Maeve was the catalyst to the supersonic explosion that had reshaped his life and refocused his future.

He would have her. He would make her his. There was no other option. Fuck letting her go her own way. Forget letting her fade into the shadows again. He refused to allow her—and that bitch Denise—ruin what could be an amazing happily ever after.

Hell. If the boys on the jobsite could hear these thoughts, they'd revoke my man card.

He snickered to himself, his gaze once again on Maeve's door, trying to peer through it to the woman on the other side.

Today. He would make his move today. He couldn't wait any longer.

There was something he had to do first, though.

Rapping his knuckles against the doorframe to Blaze's office, he waited until his friend looked up gave him a chin lift. Heading inside, he closed the door behind him.

Blaze, probably sensing something was up, threw AJ a concerned look, leaning back in his office chair.

"What's up, man?"

Dragging in a fortifying breath, AJ said, "There's something I need your help with."

chapter
EIGHTEEN

"Hey, Maeve," Blaze called to her as she was headed out the door at the end of another agonizing work week. Thankfully, AJ only stuck around until lunch that day. After that, he went off to who knew where, probably a job site. Then again, it was a Friday. He might have ducked out early to head to Miami and a long weekend with Denise.

Shutting out those thoughts, she called back to Blaze, "Yeah?"

He tossed a small white envelope at her. She caught it before it slapped her in the face.

"I know you're off, but can you drop that by AJ's? He

needs it for something he's doing this weekend, but he left it behind in his hurry to get out of here."

Yup. Definitely doing something with Denise.

Trying to not feel like a mule kicked in her the gut—and failing—she smiled at Blaze and nodded. "Sure thing. His condo isn't too far from mine."

Blaze grinned back. "He mentioned that." Raising his hand, he waved her off. "Thanks. And have a *great* weekend!"

Perplexed by her boss's weird behavior, Maeve shrugged it off. It was the weekend, the man was probably overeager to get home to his hot girlfriend and get a little something, something.

Ugh. And there went images of her and AJ from last Thursday night. The way he'd pushed her up against the brick wall and devoured her mouth. The way his hands cupped her ass, lifting her wet, aching pussy to dry hump her with his long, thick, throbbing cock through his jeans.

The near orgasm. The fumbling for answers. The abrupt end to their interlude…and her unbearable yearning to feel that alive and wanted again.

But that couldn't happen again, no matter how much Maeve prayed for it.

After a week of settling in, Callie and Lexi had become the best part of her day. Callie had pre-enrolled Lexi in school, so she was already attending Jackson Key Elementary during the day, which allowed her mom to pick up some hours at Happy Jack's with Anna. Once the day was over, though, the three of them were making up for lost time.

It had been too long since Maeve could actually sit and just talk with her best friend. Yes, Sally and Anna were great, but they didn't know the deepest parts of her. The parts that Callie knew only because she could share in the pain.

adoring **ALEJANDRO**

Both having lived in and survived stifling, emotionally and mentally abusive homes, they shared a bond Maeve wasn't willing to form with anyone else. What she and Callie shared, was special.

Maeve: Hey lady, i'm going to be late. I have to run an errand for the boss first. After that, i'll grab dinner. King noodle?

Maeve loved the ramen noodle place because it was nothing like the dried packaged stuff they sold in the stores. Callie, a self-proclaimed anime nerd, was over the moon that she had access to something she'd only read about or seen in her favorite animated Japanese shows.

Callie: Yes!

Maeve: Sake?

Callie: Heck ya!

Maeve: Get Yellowstone queued up and ready to go!

Callie: yYu don't have to tell me twice. Cowboys, rice wine, and ramen? Weird combo but just too good.

Callie had turned Maeve on to the modern cowboy drama two nights ago. Since then, they'd been binge-watching every chance they could—at least once Lexi was in bed where she couldn't be exposed to the more *adult* themes of the show.

Who the hell *didn't* want sex and violence with their cowboys?

Snickering at that thought, Maeve pointed her car in

the direction of AJ's condo, the white envelope burning a hole in her brain.

What was in it? Who was it from?

Stifling the urge to peel the damn thing open and say she got it like that, she cursed.

It wasn't any of her business, she had to remind herself. Snooping would only lead to trouble, and she'd had enough of that to last the rest of her long, lonely life.

In less time than she'd hoped, she was pulling up to AJ's condo. His massive truck was parked out in front, and the lights were illuminating the front windows.

Her heart hammering, she paused, squeezing the steering wheel until her knuckles turned white.

"I can do this," she muttered to herself. "I just need to go up there, give him the envelope, and leave. Easy peasy."

It wasn't like she had to actually have a conversation with the man. If she really wanted to be a coward, she could just slip the envelope under his door and then text him to tell him she brought it by.

Really? That's how low you've fallen? You're actually that much of a weakling that you're willing to ding-dong-ditch rather than knock on the door and face him like someone with a spine?

She groaned, dropping her forehead against the wheel. *What if Denise is there?* Tears burned her eyes, pushing for release. She allowed a few drops to escape before wiping at her cheeks furiously.

She'd put herself in the mess she was in. She could damn well deal with the consequences. Like having to face the man she loved after practically dry humping him the night before. Ugh. She was turning into such a needy slut. What could AJ think about her now? Sure, he'd been into it, too, but she could explain away that he'd been acting weird all night. The flirty text messages, the strange concern for her, then the heat of the moment when they kissed like horny teenagers about to get caught by mom and dad.

Maybe he's second guessing his couple-dom with Denise. Maybe she's already shown her true colors and AJ is looking for a way out. Yeah, and maybe AJ was just so attracted to her he just couldn't help himself and had kissed her because he loved her.

Uh huh. That's bullshit. You read that email he sent Denise this morning. He misses her. His imposter Swan. He even had a gift for her.

He's giving her gifts that should be mine! She rolled her eyes and opened the car door, snatching the envelope with purpose.

Steeling herself, she marched right up the stairs to AJ's door and knocked. Her hands shaking, she fisted them at her sides, careful not to wrinkle the precious envelope.

Sweat beaded on her forehead, her eyes staring at the door right in front of her. Suddenly, she wanted to be anywhere else but there. Her legs twitching to move, she hadn't even taken a step back before the door swung open and AJ was standing there, a panty-melting smile on his ruggedly handsome face.

"Hey," he greeted her, his voice smooth and chocolatey. "Glad you could stop by." He stepped back, his gaze drifting from her suddenly flushed face, down her body—slowly, *hungrily*—before meeting her gaze once again. "Come in."

Swaying, Maeve pressed a hand to her forehead and blinked. There was no way she saw what she thought she saw. AJ Mendez didn't just eye fuck her in his doorway.

Shaking her head to clear away the nonsense, she followed him inside and closed the door behind her, though she remained just inside the foyer. Lifting the envelope, she expected him to take it, thank her, and wave goodbye.

He did none of those things.

He turned on his heel, ignoring the envelope, and disappeared around the corner. She knew from previous visits that he was probably in the kitchen…where the delicious smells were coming from. Her mouth watered—and not just for AJ.

Her stomach grumbled, rolling. She really shouldn't have skipped breakfast. Or lunch. But the thought of eating when she was feeling so uneven had only made the sickness worse.

"I hope you like pasta because the only thing I can make that doesn't taste like burning is spaghetti," AJ called.

Stunned, Maeve blurted, "What?"

AJ's head popped around the corner. He grinned at her and winked. "Spaghetti. I hope you're hungry…because I am." He ducked back around the corner before Maeve could make sense of the suggestion in his voice.

Dragging in a breath, Maeve walked into the kitchen, stopping at the peninsula to stare at his back as he moved from stove to counter and back to the stove. The tight blue t-shirt he wore did nothing to hide the delicious movement of his back muscles as he cooked. And the jeans riding low on his waist did a fabulous job of showing off a drool-worthy ass.

Unbidden, fantasy images of that ass flexing as he thrust into her, her heels digging into the flesh of his ass cheeks as he used the packed muscle to make her come.

Her cheeks heated as desire pooled in her belly, her pussy eager for her imaginings to become reality.

Jerking her face away from him, she peered at the

six-seater dining room table and froze. It was set for two people, with candles lit in the center of the table, and a bottle of champagne chilling in a bucket beside the table.

"What's all this?" she asked, her voice thick with apprehension.

AJ turned, his gaze landing on her face, and his green eyes turning black as his lids grew heavy.

"Dinner. I figured we could both use a relaxing night."

Confused and a little bubbly with excitement, she said, "Uh huh, okay. But…why the candles? The champagne? Is…is this a…date?" Oh lordy. At that thought, heat blasted through her cheeks once more. Whether it was embarrassment or arousal, she didn't know. Probably a good dose of both.

"You looked flushed," he drawled, his voice thick. "What're you thinking about?"

Shaking her head, she forced a laugh. "I'm wondering what I'm doing here."

"I just said. Dinner."

She rolled her eyes. "Just dinner? But what about this super important thing Blaze told me you urgently needed to have tonight?" She held out the envelope once more. Without dropping his gaze from hers, he took it, tore it open, and pulled out…a sticky note?

What the hell?

Reading it, AJ barked a laugh before tossing the note on the counter and turning back to the bubbling pasta sauce on the stove.

Why had Blaze given her an envelope with a sticky note inside? Now she really wanted to know what it said. She snatched the yellow note from the counter top and turned it over.

Good luck.

Two words scrawled in Blaze's handwriting.

Good luck. For what?

Tension stiffened her limbs until they quivered, as annoyance and frustration quickly turned to anger.

She was done being the meek, uncertain, quiet, overlooked, ignored other woman. She was done with hiding behind what she wanted people to see. She was done allowing herself to be used and toyed with. Maeve couldn't tell AJ the truth about Denise, but she could damn well stop the crazy train she was on before she got hurt worse.

Denise had made her a victim, but she refused to be anything less than a woman worthy of AJ's respect.

Now, to grow some lady balls.

"What the hell is this?" she demanded angrily, tossing the note at his face when he turned toward her, his eyes wide. He hadn't expected her outburst. Oh, well, screw him.

She planted her hands on her hips and lifted her chin defiantly. "Why did Blaze have me hand deliver a note that says 'Good luck'? Why are you acting like I simply stopped in for dinner, when we both know I've been avoiding you all day? Huh?" Beyond exasperated, she threw her arms in the arm and growled.

"Aren't you hungry? I know for a fact you didn't have lunch. You were so busy avoiding me, you didn't leave your office all day."

Surprised, she huffed. "How do you know that? You left right before lunch."

Rather than answer her, AJ simply turned off the burner, moved the sauce pan to the back burner, then turned back to her, his expression unreadable. He crossed the small kitchen, slowly making his way around the counter toward where she was standing, now mute.

The man didn't walk. He stalked toward her, every inch the predator staring down his prey.

She was his prey. Trembling, she watched him, taking in the way he moved, the power in his stride, the strength in his movements. The way his muscles grew taut and flexed as he came closer and closer. He didn't stop until she was pinned against the table, the lit candles flickering from the jolt, his massive arms on either side of her, his hands gripping the edge of the table.

His eyes seared her, the hunger within his gaze devouring her.

"No more avoiding. No more hiding. No more running. This between us is fucking explosive, and I'm tired of denying myself what I know we both want."

She was shaking her head before she thought about it. "No. That's not true. You don't want me. You even said you just wanted to be friends, AJ. You want Denise—"

He pressed his forehead against hers and sneered. "Fuck Denise. This is about you and me and the fact that we've both been goddamn idiots. Yes, I said I wanted to be friends and that we should keep it friendly and professional between us, but that's all bullshit. I don't want to be your friend, Maeve, and I know you don't want to be mine."

She scoffed, surprised by her own fire. "You don't know anything."

He lifted a hand and gripped the nape of her neck. "I know more than you think."

Her fire petered out at his words as fear began to grow. What did he know?

Maeve swallowed thickly, her chest tightening. "What is it you think you know?"

He leaned in closer, his mouth brushing against hers. She could feel the heat of his breath on her face, the press of his body against hers. His hardness. Her softness. Need flooded her, making her gasp.

Against her trembling lips, he whispered, "I know I need to fuck you, baby. Right here. Right now. Just the two of us. No one else. Stop thinking. Feel this—" he ground his long, thick erection against her belly— "feel me. Be with me, Maeve. Stop denying this. Stop hiding."

Stop hiding.
Stop running.
Just for tonight.
Feel.

With a groan torn from the depths of her chest, she threw her arms around his neck and melted into him.

"For tonight."

Without another word, AJ took her hand, and she followed behind him.

She'd follow him wherever he led.

chapter
NINETEEN

HER HEAD FILLED WITH SCREAMING THOUGHTS, SHE didn't even bother looking at his room. Her eyes were caught dead on the king-sized bed, though. The sheets were gray and the comforter was navy blue. The pillows were a perfect mix of navy and gray. Perfectly, utterly masculine. Just like AJ.

His hand still wrapped around hers, he pulled her up beside the bed and stopped.

Instead of dropping her hand, he placed it against his chest, leaned in, and kissed her.

Her heart turned over and began pounding away. The heavy, thundering beats rushing through her ears. She could hear nothing but her heart, but she could feel his mouth as he commanded hers, taking her moans of pleasure into his own throat.

AJ broke the kiss, dragging sharp breaths into his heaving chest.

"Fuck, I need to get you naked. I need to be inside you."

Delirious, she answered, "Yes." No other words formed in her brain.

Reaching back, AJ pulled his shirt from his body, revealing a chest Maeve had only ever envisioned in her dreams. The hard plains of his chest made her mouth water, and the ridges and valleys of his abs begged for her hands. Before she could touch him there, though, he began unbuttoning her blouse. With each button undone, her anxiety rose. Yes, she wanted to know the pleasure of being with AJ. No, she didn't want the humiliation of him seeing her naked…and ultimately rejecting her.

"I can hear your thoughts, baby, and you're wrong. I want to see all of this gorgeous, curvy flesh with my own eyes. I want to touch you, taste you, feel you beneath me as I fuck you deep and hard. Don't hide all this lush beauty from me. I need to see you."

Struck mute, she stared up at him, unable to believe he meant it. But there, as plain as day, was the dark, hot, wicked desire in his eyes.

Desire for her.

Fat Maeve.

Loosening her body, she allowed him to remove her shirt, then drag down the zipper in her skirt until she stood before him in only her black boy short panties and her plain black cotton bra. If she'd known she was going to live out her greatest fantasy that night, she could have at least worn her going out bra.

With a shove, Maeve fell backward onto AJ's bed with a yelp. Pushing up on to her elbows, she watched, her mouth hanging open, as AJ removed his jeans and then his boxer briefs.

Naked. AJ was naked. And erect. She stared at him, in all his taut, tanned, marble-carved glory, and drooled. Each muscle was perfectly defined, rippling beneath his skin with each minute movement.

She wasn't a virgin, she'd had sex that one time with the guy who'd taken her to prom—she was the cliché. But right then, staring at the most beautiful cock she'd ever imagined, she felt waaaay out of her depth. Long, straight, thick, its puffy mushroom head a deep, angry red.

God, she needed that dick inside her!

AJ knelt on the bed, crawling over her, shifting her body, until he was nestled in the cradle of her thighs. His erection thick and heavy against her womanhood. With one hand, he drew her right leg up until it was wrapped around him, then he did the same with the left, until he was so close to her, so flush with her, she could feel his pulse through his cock.

Her hands shaking, she slid her hands up his chest and over his shoulders, then back again. Simply touching him made her body tight and liquid pool in her center. She was so damp, there was no way he couldn't feel her need for him.

"Tonight, you are mine, Maeve. If you don't want this, say something now, because once I start, there is no going back." Bending his head, he nipped at her bottom lip, making her moan. He did it again, and with each nip, her hips bucked up, thrusting against his pulsing hardness.

"I want you," she breathed, unable to articulate just how

much she wanted him. With every cell of her body and every fiber of her being, she wanted him. He peered down into her face with eyes of emerald fire.

"And you'll have me."

With a deft flick, he removed her bra. His gaze took in her swollen, aching breasts with a wicked, leering smile.

"As beautiful and perfect as I imagined they'd be. Your nipples are the color of *cherries*, Maeve." He chuckled, deep and grumbly.

He kissed his way down her body, from her neck, to her collarbone, down the center of her chest, to her soft, not-flat belly, and toward the wet, aching parts of her. Taking his time as though to savor the taste, she could only feel.

She was *all* feeling.

Shifting, AJ drew her panties down her legs and tossed them to the floor, before cradling himself between her thighs once more, his broad shoulders holding her legs apart.

Kissing his way from the apex of her pussy to the inside of her thigh, he nipped the flesh there, making her jerk and moan from the pain-pleasure.

"AJ, oh God," she whimpered.

He drew in a deep breath and groaned. "Fuck, you smell delicious, I need to taste you on my tongue. I need to make you come so you fill my mouth with your sticky cream."

He lapped at her, dragging his tongue from her entrance to her clit before flicking the throbbing ball of nerves. He flattened his tongue, pressing in until no part of her cunt went untasted. He pursed his lips around her clit and nipped it with his teeth. She shuddered as he sucked.

"Give it to me, Maeve. Come in my mouth so I can fuck you and make you come on my cock," he demanded thickly, his own need evident.

adoring ALEJANDRO

Her body, his slave, did as he commanded. Her release shattered through her, making her cry out harshly. And as she shook with each jolt of pleasure, he continued lapping at her, feasting on her, until she melted into the bed, boneless.

He chuckled, rising above her. Her wetness glistening on his chin and mouth.

"You taste so fucking good," he growled then bent down and took her mouth in a devastating kiss. She could taste her own orgasm, and it turned her over, making her need rise once more.

Cupping her breasts, he took a nipple in his mouth and sucked hard. She quaked from the sensation. He nursed, sucking and nibbling, pouring his attention into one breast while his other hand slid between her thighs to work her clit. Pleasure rolled through her, blocking out everything but AJ and what he was going to her body. He switched to her other nipple, giving it his rabid attention. Her clit throbbed, pulsing as he pinched it, rubbed it.

His voice black silk, he said, "Put my cock inside you."

Needing him inside her as much as she needed her next breath, she reached for him. His thickness jumped in her hand, making her gasp.

He chuckled darkly. "He likes you."

She moaned, placing the head of him at her entrance. She'd only had sex the one time, and his dick was nowhere near as big as AJ. She knew AJ would fit, but it would be a tight fit.

Brushing her hair from her forehead, he peered down into her eyes once more, lust and yearning flared in the depths of his eyes…and so did something she couldn't possibly believe.

Stroking his back, she braced herself, tensing for his delicious invasion.

"Relax for me, baby. Let me in," he cooed, pushing his cock head into her. He groaned, tossing his head back to moan into the ceiling. The cords of his throat working as he continued impaling her, inch by inch.

So full.

So tight.

"Fuck, Maeve. You feel so fucking good! Perfect, so fucking perfect."

Finally, he bottomed out, his balls shifting against her ass. He paused, dropping his head to look down at where they were joined. She followed his gaze and nearly came.

His thick cock was stretching her, the sight practically offensive in its blatant sexual imagery. He was inside her, penetrating to the very depths of her.

"Move, please move!" she begging, writhing.

Guiding her legs higher, he changed the angle of his penetration, making her pussy convulse.

"Fuck!" they both cried out at the same time.

Pulling out to the tip, he slowly pushed into her, inch by scalding inch of scorching flesh inside her. She watched while her body took him, swallowing him, until their groins collided. Never in her life had she felt something so devastatingly intense, as though she couldn't breathe without him there, inside her, moving within her.

Lifting her hips, she met him, thrust for thrust, until they'd created a rhythm, an external heartbeat to which they pounded out their pleasure.

Sweat beaded on his forehead, dropping on to her tits as they bounced with each of his increasingly forceful thrusts.

And then, suddenly, she erupted, the world going black,

all of her senses, all pleasure, all sensation a pin point of brilliant light behind her eyes. She screamed, her core squeezing, rippling.

Above her, AJ sped up, his hips slamming into her, the sounds of hot flesh slapping against flesh interspersed with his grunts and her whimpers as he powered into her. Thrusting deeper, pounding harder and faster, until—

"Maeve!" he roared, his great big body bending backward as his cock jerked in time with his release, his thick seed rocketing into her welcoming cunt as she came with such power, she could feel his heart racing through the vein in his cock.

AJ collapsed on her, his weight delicious.

Their chests slamming together as they both fought to breathe, there was nothing to say. No words in any language that could fill the silence already heavy with weighted emotions.

Slowly, AJ pulled out of her and slipped from the bed toward the bathroom.

Sometime during their foreplay, he'd thought to put on a condom. Good. She hadn't even been thinking about that.

Her body replete, her mind quiet and still for the first time in years, Maeve rolled over and snuggled into the comforter. She felt AJ as he slid into bed beside her.

"Get a quick nap, but after that, I'm going to have you again."

He didn't have to tell her twice. She closed her eyes, curled her body around his, and….

She awoke just as the light from a new morning slipped over her face.

AJ was on his side facing away from her, so slinking from the bed like a bandit was easier than she expected.

Tonight….

One night with the man she loved…and it had been unspeakably amazing.

The shame she expected to feel wasn't there, instead she felt regret. She regretted that their one and only night together was over. She regretted that she'd been too much of a coward to reveal herself as Swan that night of the holiday party, because if she had, Denise would never have had the opportunity to get her claws into AJ. She regretted that AJ could never be hers, no matter how deeply she yearned for him.

Yes, she had regrets, but she would never be ashamed of the shared pleasure she'd experienced last night with the man she loved.

Her vision blurry with tears, she scribbled a note on a piece of paper and left it on the counter beside the bowl of cold, hard pasta they hadn't gotten around to eating last night. The table held guttered candles she hadn't gotten to enjoy. The champagne sat unopened in a bucket of water.

AJ had planned a dinner date.

But they hadn't had the date nor dinner part.

Because they'd been too busy fucking each other's brains out to stop and eat. They'd been hungry, ravenous for each other. After texting Callie to tell her she wasn't going to be home, leaving the bed had never crossed Maeve's mind. Nor AJ's—if the number of condoms they'd gone through was any indication.

No.

Stop!

She couldn't think about that. She couldn't think about the fact that she'd had sex with a man who belonged to someone else, even if that someone else was her enemy.

Grabbing her purse and keys from where she'd

apparently dropped them just inside AJ's condo, she hurried to her car.

Numb and yet overwhelmed with all she was feeling, she made it to her own condo and into the shower before the flood of tears cascaded over the dam.

She didn't know how long she stood under the water sobbing, but once the water ran cold, she dried off, robotically went about putting on her clothes, brushing her teeth, and pulling her hair back.

It was a Saturday, which meant she had two full days before she had to face AJ again.

That was two full days to sink into the memories of last night and catalog each and every scent, sensation, taste, moan, gasp, sigh, ache, pain, and pleasure. Because once Monday arrived, AJ was untouchable.

chapter
TWENTY

SHE'D RUN FROM HIM AGAIN. FRIDAY NIGHT HAD BEEN the best night of his life. Taking Maeve, pleasuring her, finally having her in his arms and his bed…. It had been a fantasy come to life. But, in the bright light of a Florida morning, she was gone.

At least she'd had the courtesy of leaving a note.

A bullshit note that said their night together had been a mistake. That they couldn't do that again because Maeve didn't want to be the "other woman."

Fuck that. There was no other woman for AJ.

He'd sent dozens of texts, left her voice messages, and had even knocked on her apartment door, demanding she answer. He wasn't done with her. He would never be done with her, but he knew she needed time to wrap her head around their new reality.

She was his, but she was fighting it. Once she knew that *he* knew she was Swan, things would get easier.

Right?

It had taken every ounce of his willpower to head into work, stride past her office, and sit down at his own desk in his office across from hers without racing to Maeve, pulling her into his arms, and admitting he knew the truth about her as Swan.

But he couldn't. Not yet. She was withdrawing, pulling in to herself, hiding once again. If he admitted the truth, she'd run for the hills. She wasn't ready for the intensity that would come when he finally had her all to himself.

No. He had to take his time, get her used to the idea of being with him. She'd hidden behind the persona of Swan so long, she didn't know how to handle him as Maeve.

He didn't blame her; he was a lot to handle. He smirked at his own thoughts, casting his gaze across the corridor to the woman huddled behind her desk. She was wearing brown again, like a shield.

His cock stirring, he bit back the urge to tear the shield from her body and invade.

He sat like that, hard as a rock, for hours, trying to concentrate on all the paperwork he'd been putting off for weeks.

Maeve, in her own world, distracted by whatever she was thinking, didn't notice him watching her. Like a fucking creep. But what other choice did he have? As soon as she noticed him, she'd make some excuse to leave. She'd returned to the skittish mouse she'd been all the months before. This time, however, he knew just how amazing the fiery vixen could be.

No, he knew how amazing and wonderful his Swan could be. When she wasn't hiding her true self.

His own thoughts were disturbed by the email notification sound coming from Maeve's computer. Heaving a sigh, Maeve clicked…and her entire expression drained from her face, along with all color.

An email notification from his own computer sounded, but he couldn't look away from whatever was happening across the hall in Maeve's office. What was in that email that had made her look like that? Had something happened?

His phone ringing jerked him back to his own office.

Dropping his gaze from Maeve, he picked up his cell and noticed Denise's name on the screen. Scowling at it, he silenced it. Like a magnet, his gaze was drawn back to Maeve's office. Which was now empty.

Where had she gone?

Checking the clock, he noticed it was only a few minutes before the end of the work day. Perhaps Maeve had hurried off to deal with whatever was in that email.

Unsettled, AJ gathered his shit and headed out.

At home, after his shower, he poured himself two fingers of Jameson and leaned against the railing of his balcony. The balcony off his bedroom looked out over a sandy rise that, at one time, had been a sand dune rimmed with palisades. Now that the ocean and hurricanes had reshaped the land, it was simply a rise now home to rootless weeds.

It wasn't the best view, but it was better than no view at all. Like at Maeve's.

Maeve. Was she okay?

Something niggled at him, digging in and burrowing

adoring **ALEJANDRO**

deep. Whatever was in that email was enough to utterly cripple the woman. He'd seen the way her eyes grew large, her skin paled, and her breathing shuddered. He couldn't miss the way her whole body seemed to collapse in on itself as fear filled her eyes.

A thought prickled, and he latched on to it, pulling his phone from his pocket.

AJ: Hey man, do you have access to employee emails?

Blaze: I have admin access. You do, too. Why?

Hurrying to his laptop, he logged into the company email server, typed in his credentials, and looked for the appropriate tab.

There! Employee email access. As the boss, he had access to all email accounts on the business server. He wasn't doing anything wrong—and if his suspicions were correct, he would be doing something to right an already terrible wrong.

Scrolling through the list of employees, he found Maeve's name and clicked on it.

Ignoring all the emails dated yesterday, he found one sent from Denise's account to Maeve's that afternoon. What could Denise have sent to Maeve that would have terrified Maeve like that? And why?

He clicked.

And the world dropped out from beneath him.

Screen shots of Facebook accounts for Maeve, Callie, Sally, Sylvester, Anna, and Blaze. There was also what looked like a yearbook picture of third-grade Lexi. The only one missing was AJ. Beneath each screenshot was a link. Hand trembling, he clicked the link beneath Sally's picture.

The link led to a secured landing page with a detailed

list of what could only be described as a list of intentional calamities.

> **Drain bank accounts**
> **Photoshop pictures of her fucking another man**
> **Sell those pics online**
> **Create criminal record for drug distribution**
> **Create arrest warrant**
> **Call the police with anonymous tip**

"What the fuck?" he spat, nausea rising into his throat. It was like a hit list on his sister. His motherfucking *sister*!

Clicking out of Sally's list, he clicked on Maeve's, anger and dread sinking him fast. As he read, his anger grew, morphing into rage. Denise had it all planned out—she was going to turn Maeve into some kind of child predator with terrorist ties.

On and on the links beneath the screen shots revealed more and more of Denise's terrifying and disgusting threats. And he didn't need to wonder why the woman was threatening to ruin so many people. The words in bold cross the top of the email revealed much.

Tell AJ the truth & this will all become a reality. Keep your mouth shut and you'll all be safe.

The woman had found Maeve's emails to AJ as Swan. But what was her endgame? What was the purpose for the lying and the threats? AJ was arrogant enough to admit women went crazy over him, but crazy enough to create such an elaborate scheme, and then to threaten such horrendous things on people AJ loved?

She had to be stopped.

Grabbing his phone, he called the only person who could help him fuck with a woman who had far too much power.

"AJ?" Sly's voice rumbled over the line.

"Sly, man, you need to get here now. Don't tell Sally."

There was a moment of silence where AJ knew Sly was contemplating the hurt he'd be in if Sally realized he'd kept something from her once again. Finally, he sighed and replied, "I'll be right there."

"What the fuck is this shit?" Blaze roared, throwing his beer bottle against the wall where it shattered into uncountable pieces. "What the fuck is wrong with Denise? Why would she threaten all this shit?"

After calling Sly, AJ had called Blaze. With both men and their respective women involved, he knew they would want to know what was going on. And AJ could use all the help he could get.

"That's what I want to know. Why does my director of IT have it out for Sally?" Sly growled, his protective instincts for AJ's sister rising. "What the hell did Maeve do?"

"Maeve didn't do shit. She's on that list, too. This is Denise threatening Maeve. You can read it yourself. If Maeve opens her mouth, Denise will unleash all that shit on Maeve and our friends and family."

"What is Maeve supposed to keep quiet about? What can she possibly know that is so important that Denise is threatening to turn the woman I love into a drug kingpin?" Sly demanded, his face ruddy with unspent anger.

"Swan," AJ replied.

Blaze stiffened and Sly jerked, his eyes glaring a hole through AJ.

"This is about your online woman? Are you fucking serious right now?" Blaze sneered, rising to his full height, his hands in fists at his sides. "You better explain right now, brother, because I am about out of patience."

"You know that I've been emailing back and forth with a woman I'd named Swan—she without a name. Well, things got serious between us pretty quickly, because…well, there was something about her that drew me in. I wanted her. I wanted to meet her, to bring her into my life and take things to the next level."

Sly sneered. "That's some Dateline Special shit, AJ."

AJ couldn't help it, he cracked a smile. "That's exactly what Sally said."

Sly snorted, cracking is own grin. "I bet." His grin fell away as he asked, "So, Denise showed up, right? Saying she was Swan?"

"She did. The thing is, right from the beginning, I had my suspicions. The woman in the emails and the woman presented to me, didn't feel like the same person, but what proof did I have that Denise wasn't who she said she was? I couldn't help but wonder if Swan really was Denise and I was just being picky."

"We all know Denise, man. If you're bitch alarm was going off, it should have been enough to nip that shit in the bud," Blaze pointed out unhelpfully.

"I know that when I first realized she was claiming to be Swan, my first instinct was to run like hell. But then what happened if I ran, and I ruined my shot at having the woman I'd been falling for?" Fuck, he sounded like a pussy-whipped shit stain, but there was nothing for it. He needed to be open and honest with the two men he trusted the most in the world.

"So, you're saying that she isn't Swan, that she was lying—wait!" Sly barked, slapping his forehead and reeling. "You mean Maeve—*my* Maeve—is your Swan?"

Possessiveness jerked to the surface as he grumbled, "*My* Maeve, *my* Swan."

Chuckling, Sly raised his hands placatingly. "All yours, man."

"If Maeve is Swan, why didn't she stop Denise when she came into the office hanging all over you, claiming to be her?"

"My guess is that, at first, Maeve was shocked. Wouldn't you be if someone came in claiming to be you right in front of you?"

Both Sly and Blaze nodded thoughtfully.

"After that, I'm assuming, is when Denise first threatened Maeve to keep her quiet. That first week, Maeve was practically a shadow of herself, super skittish, looking like she was sicker than a dog but still coming in to work."

"I noticed that, too. I just assumed she was sick, but that she was so dedicated to her work, she didn't take the time off." Blaze cursed. "I should have paid more attention. I should have checked on her, made sure she was okay."

"She would have just lied to you. Denise's threats are next level, man." Sly sat down at AJ's table and pulled the laptop toward him to click through the email again. "What the hell was Denise thinking? This email, if Maeve wanted to take this to the cops, Denise would be in deep shit."

AJ, shaking his head, replied, "Denise is an IT genius. She could make all of this shit go away before the cops could even pull their heads out of their asses, and, by then, she'd have implemented enough of her plan to hurt Maeve for crossing her."

"Can't you lock her out of the White systems?" Blaze asked.

"She built most of those systems, she can backdoor whatever we put in place, and fuck us hard."

"So, we just let Maeve live under threat while Denise gets to ride into the sunset with AJ?"

AJ growled, hatred fueling his fire. "That woman will never touch me again. If I had my way, she'd already be buried up to her neck, just before high tide. Thank God I never fucked her. I'd have to cut off my dick and burn it."

All three of them hissed, wincing.

"I know a guy," Sly interjected, leaning back in his seat with a hard look on his face. "I've been trying to recruit him for White for years now. He currently works for a private security firm in Vegas running their cyber security department, tracing black hat motherfuckers, and digging up shit on terrorists. The man is a genius with the keyboard, but he's also deadly with a sniper rifle."

"You think he'll help?" AJ asked, hope surging beneath the surface of fear.

"For the right price, yeah."

"I'll pay anything."

Sly cursed, pushing to his feet to punch the table with a meaty fist. "Fuck that. That bitch threatened Sally. I'll make sure Samson gets whatever the hell he wants. You can count on that."

Slumping against the counter, the strength leaching from his body, AJ closed his eyes and sighed.

Blaze's confident voice cut through the weary fog in AJ's mind.

adoring **ALEJANDRO**

"We're going to get her, AJ. Maeve will be safe. The question is, what are you going to do once this is all over?"

Good question.

Opening his eyes, he met Blaze's worried gaze, then Sly's resolute one. Both men had come when he called. Relief blossomed inside him, as the burdened he'd carried was lifted by two others.

It was time to get his woman—and put Denise down.

"Right. So, this Samson, he can make sure that Denise is locked down, that she can't follow through with her threats?"

Smirking darkly, Sly nodded. "Without a doubt. I'll text him now." Silence filled the condo as Sly's thumbs flew over his phone screen. "Once Denise is locked down and can't do her cyber voodoo, we're going to need to gather the information and get the FBI involved. With the kind of threats she made, this is federal. We'll need local PD help at first, though. That new detective, Oliveira, seems keen on doing his job right."

How Sly knew so much about a local police detective, AJ didn't know—and probably didn't want to.

Blaze huffed. "What should I do? I can't just sit around waiting for someone else to save my woman."

AJ chuckled, slapping Blaze on the back. "You're going to help me catch my Swan."

A joyful whoop sounded and Blaze and AJ turned to a brilliantly grinning Sly.

"Samson is in. Let's do this!"

His heart in his throat, it beating a mile a minute, AJ gripped his cell with both hands. Taking a deep breath, he peered down at the screen and typed out a one sentence message.

AJ: Baby, it'd love to see you this weekend.

The words like nails on a chalkboard, making his jaw hurt from grinding his teeth. Denise wasn't his baby, she was his bane. His enemy, and soon, she'd be history. Forgotten. Left to die in a cell as dank and rotten as her.

It didn't take long for the viperous bitch to respond.

Denise: I'm on my way.

Dark fire scorched through him, lighting every last sliver of righteous tinder ablaze. The smile on his face wide, vicious, and malevolent.

"Hey Sly?" AJ called.

Sly arched an eyebrow. "Yeah?"

"Feel like buying out a bar for a night?"

adoring **ALEJANDRO**

From the Desk of AJ Mendez to Maeve Thomas

January 21st

My Swan, you ready to stop hiding?
Meet me @ Happy Jack's. 7pm. Tonight.
Wear the red dress.

Forever yours,
AJ

chapter
TWENTY-ONE

MAEVE SCOWLED DOWN AT THE EMAIL THAT HAD JUST come through on her cell. To her personal email account. The one *not* attached to her anonymous SWAN account where she usually received the Swan emails.

It was from AJ. To her *personal account*.

But...he'd called her Swan. On her *personal* email.

Pinching her forehead, she furiously tried to gather her suddenly frenzied thoughts.

If AJ was sending her a personal email and calling her Swan, did that mean...?

He knew she was Swan.

He knew the truth she'd been hiding.

Oh shit! What about Denise?

What about Denise? He emailed you at your personal email and called you Swan. He knows Denise isn't Swan.

Joy surged, propelled by hope, fueled by relief...but then fear arrived like a case of shingles.

If Denise didn't get AJ, what did that mean for her threats? Would she still implement those terrible plans in that email? Denise was a spiteful bitch, Maeve wouldn't put it past her to fuck with Maeve just to get a thrill out of it. To see Maeve crumble and fall at her hand.

If Maeve met up with AJ, would Denise find out and blame Maeve for losing her chance at AJ's money?

Dread and panic coiled together in her belly as bile rose into her throat and mouth. She tried to swallow away the acrid sourness, but her belly kept churning, and churning.

Did she go and finally face AJ for the chance at a happily ever after, or did she allow her fear of what Denise might do keep her from having the life Denise had been intent on stealing?

Stop hiding....

Was it that easy?

When is anything with love that easy?

The email had said seven tonight. She glanced at the clock, her heart hammering.

That was only one hour away.

She'd taken the day off of work since both Blaze and AJ had sent notice that they'd be out of the office all day. So, she'd taken a "me" day to write up her resignation letter.

She was leaving Harris Construction, LLC. She couldn't stomach spending her days watching as AJ and Denise got closer. As the woman who stole everything from her lived the life Maeve should have. As bad as it hurt already, Maeve couldn't fathom the pain she'd endure when AJ proposed to Denise, married Denise, and they eventually started a family.

Little caramel-skinned, dark-haired angels, with their father's beautiful green eyes.

A sob shook her, tearing a sound of pure anguish from her throat.

No. That future was hers.

Quickly throwing on the red dress, shoving her feet in black flats, and tossing her hair into a ponytail, she hurried to make herself even slightly presentable to the man she was going to risk it all for.

No more hiding.

No more running.

She wasn't a mouse, she was a vixen.

She was AJ's Swan.

And it was time to finally claim him as hers.

Just as he'd already claimed her heart.

By the time she pulled her car up to Happy Jack's she was thrumming with unspent nervous energy. She was so caught up in her thoughts it took her a moment to realize... that parking lot was empty. On a Thursday night.

"That's not weird," she mumbled to herself while getting out of her car. Yeah, it was weird, but AJ said to be there, so there she was.

Dragging in a long, slow breath of humid evening air, she pulled on the handle, opening the door, and striding inside. Shoulders back, head up, eyes wide.

No more hiding.

The place was a ghost town.

Empty.

Except for the gorgeous man standing in the middle of the room.

Dressed in a simple light blue button down, it's long sleeves barely containing his shoulders and arms. The material stretched across his chest, and was tucked in around his trim waist. His long, thick legs were encased in a pair of dark designer jeans. On his feet were shiny black dress shoes. She dragged her gaze from his hard, tight body to take in the rest of him. And he stood there, letting her look her fill.

His black hair was styled, his naturally wavy locks brushed to one side and a single large curl looped over his forehead. His slight five o'clock shadow framed a face so handsome, she sighed. His green eyes were bright and intense, staring at her, waiting for her.

Tension roiled through her, tightening her chest.

Speak!

"Where is everyone?"

He laughed, rubbing at the back of neck nervously, a coy smile on his beautiful face. "Sly did me a favor. I wanted us to be alone someplace we both enjoyed."

"Well, um…I'm here," she bleated, nerves stealing the iron from her voice.

He smirked, taking a step toward her. "I can see that. Thank you for coming."

"We're you scared I wouldn't?"

He took another step closer and chuckled. Warmed by the sound, she took a step closer to him, her body hungry to be near his. Drawn to him as she always was.

"Actually, I was terrified. I had no idea if you'd actually get the email, or that you'd even read it. After all the shit I've done to you, how I've made you feel, I was almost certain you'd block me and tell me to fuck off."

Step in step with one another, they finally stopped beside the bar. A lonely box sat there.

Her heart ached for him, his words hitting her deep. He was as twisted up as she was.

"I wouldn't do that—well, the blocking part. I've definitely cursed your name a few times already today."

He nodded, a wry grin on his face. "I don't blame you. I've wanted to punch myself a few times this week. Thankfully, Blaze and Sly were there to do it for me."

She snorted, laughing. "Why aren't there any bruises?"

He chuckled, shrugging. "They're under the clothes."

Spears of heat pierced her, filling her with dark want. She knew, intimately, what was beneath his clothes, and from the way his eyes grew heavy, he remembered what was under hers, too.

"Hold that thought," he said huskily, thrusting the white box into her hand. Startled, she took it, staring down at it with wide eyes. Perplexed and yet utterly curious, she lifted her gaze to his. "I meant to give this to you this last Friday night, but…well, things got a little carried away."

Remembering just what he meant, her core throbbed. She clenched her thighs together to stave off the worst of it, and barely met his gaze.

When she did, all needful heat rushed from her body.

Fear. Uncertainty. His eyes were glimmering with a vulnerability she'd seen only once before…that first day she'd seen him for the first time. He didn't know anyone was looking, but she watched him as he watched a newly married couple who were in the office to conference about their home build. AJ looked at them like they had all the answers in the universe. In that moment, Maeve had witnessed him unguarded. Raw, broken.

And right now, AJ, the beautiful, strong, confident man before her…was uncertain. Scared. Of what?

Holding her breath, she pried open the box lid and pulled something from the nest of white tissue paper. Realizing what was in her hand, she couldn't help the bark of laughter.

"A mug?" she laughed. "You bought me a mug." The mug was pure white and just the perfect size for a 16oz coffee—just like she liked.

AJ grinned and took the empty box from her, placing it on the bar top. "Turn it over. Read the other side. I hope you like it."

"Oh." There was more?

Carefully, she turned the mug over…and nearly dropped it.

There, right there before her eyes, was the imprinted image of two swans, their beaks touching, their regal necks curled into the shape of a heart. Beneath the image, a quote.

Being deeply loved by someone gives you strength.
Loving someone deeply gives you courage.
—Lao Tzu

She stared, reading and re-reading the quote beneath the striking image of a mated pair of swans. Tears prickled the backs of her eyes, demanding to be spilled, to burn a river down her cheeks.

She gasped, shuddering. "AJ?" She dragged her gaze from the mug and met his eyes.

Love. Love burned there in brilliant emerald green.

"What does this mean? You know…."

He was there, gripping her head in his hands, pressing his forehead against hers to peer down into her flushed face.

"You are my Swan. My love. The one who gives me

courage. The one who brought me to life when I'd been dead inside for so long. You, Maeve, are everything I'd ever wanted for myself but never dared believe I deserved."

Gripping the mug tightly, she held it against her chest as if to absorb it into her being.

Without looking away from AJ's raw and intense gaze, she effused, "You deserve everything, AJ. You are the most amazing man I've ever known—and I've known some assholes."

He smiled sadly, closing his eyes for a moment before opening them again. A sorrow shone there that wasn't there before.

"We chatted so much in those emails, and I really wanted to tell you everything, to share all the ugliness of my life with you, but…. There's things about me you don't know, Maeve. Things I haven't had the courage to tell you until now."

Pulling back just enough to see his whole face, Maeve tipped her head to the side and asked, "Like what?"

There wasn't a damn thing he could tell her that would make her think less of him.

Carefully placing the mug on the bar beside its box, Maeve flattened her palms against his chest. His wildly beating heart was slamming against his chest. Whatever it was that he had to tell her terrified him.

"Tell me, AJ," she murmured against his lips, her own courage pushing her to touch him, comfort him, show him that she was there for him when he needed her.

AJ sighed, closing his eyes once more, cutting her off from the clear view of his vulnerability and fear. Pulling her fully against him—chest to chest—he pressed a soft kiss to her temple, breathing deep.

adoring **ALEJANDRO**

Finally, he spoke.

"My father was a cheating asshole who only cared about his money and getting his dick wet. He didn't even try to hide his affairs from my mother, throwing his other women in her face, fucking them in their bed, flaunting his hatred for his wife and his marriage wherever he went."

Maeve gasped, disgusted. "Why even get married?"

AJ grunted. "Money. My mom's dowry was a company my dad wanted. So, he romanced, seduced, and then married my mom. As soon as the ink was dry on the legal documents, my dad couldn't get away fast enough. The thing was, though, my mom actually loved my dad. She'd fallen hard for him." He laughed humorlessly. "What you've got to understand about my mother was that, when she loved, she loved hard. She fell for my dad's lies, and she gave all of herself to him. Her body, her heart, her soul. She loved him deeply, and no matter how terribly he treated her, she stayed with him."

"Oh, AJ…." What else could she say? The woman obviously married the wrong man, but if she hadn't, AJ and Sallina wouldn't have happened. "What happened?" Because she just knew something did.

AJ pressed another long, soft kiss to her temple and sighed. "She drank to numb the pain. Sally dealt with the brunt of that, though. And that's her story to tell. But, for me, that pain, my mother's pain, was something that hit me hard. When she committed suicide, the one thing I thought more than anything else was that her love was wasted on a man who didn't deserve it. That my mother's deeply loving heart was given to the wrong person, someone who couldn't appreciate the beauty he'd been given. And I swore, standing over her grave, that I would never be like my father. If I ever found a love like my mother felt for my father, I would cherish it. I would hold on to it, and I would make sure I lived and loved worthy of it."

AJ dropped his arms and pulled away just as the sounds of a car door slamming fractured their moment.

She glanced at the door then back at AJ. "What's happening?"

"Maeve," he breathed, reaching out to caress her overwarm cheek with his thumb. "This is me, being worthy of it."

"What—"

Before she could ask him what the hell he meant, the doors to the empty bar swung open.

Denise Walters sauntered in.

chapter
TWENTY-TWO

AJ watched the confusion then panic fill Maeve's eyes. God, what he would give to shield her from what was about to happen, but he couldn't. She needed to be there, to bear witness to something required of him as the man who loved her.

Love.

He fucking loved the shit out of her.

And now, he would prove it the only way he could.

Tearing his gaze from his Maeve, he turned to Denise, who was glaring at Maeve like she was shit on her four inch heels.

"Denise," he cooed, nearly throwing up in his mouth.

He needed to make sure Denise focused on him, even if it meant hurting Maeve in the short term. "Baby, I'm glad you could make it."

A sharp intake of breath made AJ wince. He couldn't look at Maeve or he'd crumble, and their well-laid plans could fail. He needed to keep Denise there, at Happy Jack's, until he got the signal from Sly.

Come on, Sly. Hurry the fuck up.

While Denise was with him, Sly's man, Samson was hacking into Denise's phone, wiping it, and blocked her access to White's systems where all her threatening materials were stored. The woman was so fucking arrogant, she didn't even consider keeping her blackmail shit on a private server. She believed she was untouchable, that no one would ever be able to best her. Well, Samson Wellington, former Naval Intelligence and SEAL, was set to prove her wrong.

Strutting toward him, her hips swaying, Denise looked every inch the beautiful poison. Pretty but venomous. She'd dressed in a short, tight black dress that looked like it should have been a bandage rather than evening wear.

As she neared him, he held himself in place. The urge to take a step back, to put space between her and his body, was so great, he had to bite the inside of his cheek to keep himself standing there.

Her painted lips curled into a seductive grin and her eyes grew hooded, her gaze dropping to drag over him, taking in his body. He wanted to wanted to scrub his flesh until he was raw.

"Baby, what is she doing here?" she asked, snarling at Maeve over her shoulder. Maeve, his strong, beautiful Maeve, didn't even flinch.

That's it, baby, just keep watching. I'll fix this all for you.

Just then, his cell buzzed in his pocket. Then again in quick succession. Sly's signal.

It was time.

"Huh. Didn't you get my text?" he asked, innocence dripping from his tongue.

She furrowed her brow and pursed her lips, clearly confused. Raising her arm, she reached into her tiny, beaded purse.

He hadn't sent her a text, but she wouldn't know that. But she *would* know something else in three…two…one…

"What the fuck?" Denise barked, scowling down at her cell. All the pretty pretense twisting into ugly truth on her face.

"Is something wrong?" he asked, not even bothering to keep the condescension from his tone.

Her focus snapped to him, her eyes narrowing sharply. "You did this! What the fuck did you do to my phone?"

"I didn't do anything to your phone, Denise. I wouldn't have any idea what it takes to wipe a cellphone and destroy every piece of information stored on it." At her gasp, he continued, shrugging. "I wouldn't have the first clue how to download all the data, upload it to an encrypted server, and then send that information to the FBI. Oh, and I wouldn't know how to restrict all access to the White servers so you couldn't even back door them no matter what you tried."

She was vibrating by that point, her phone gripped so hard in her hand, it would probably break any moment.

Panting, her face three shades of blistering red, she shrilled, "What the fuck did you do?"

Annnnnd, that was the cue for the other players in their Destroy Denise scheme to make their appearance.

Maeve, still standing there, her hands cupping her

mouth, her eyes wide and filled with disbelief, turned to look at the door to the kitchen as it swung open and Blaze, Sly, Samson, and a new player, Detective Camilo Oliveira from the Jackson Key police department, strode into the room.

Damn it was getting crowded...and intense.

Beside him, Denise tensed, her body going ramrod straight.

"Sylvester, what are you doing here?" she spluttered, clearly feeling the noose closing around her neck.

He glared at her, sneering, "I'm here because, apparently, someone I trusted with the security of my business targeted my friends and my woman with nasty threats."

Denise turned white as a sheet. "You can't mean me, Sylvester. I've only ever been loyal to you. Your company's security is important to me, why would I target anyone?"

AJ clucked his tongue, jerking her attention back to him. He could see the panic settling in, and the desperation beginning to rise.

"It seems as though you set your sights on me and all my money, isn't that right? You saw the emails between Maeve and I, and you decided you were going to cash in, sliding in to claim you were Swan to get your greedy hands on me and my wallet."

She shook her head violently. "No, that's not true. I love *you*, AJ. Your money means nothing to me."

He laughed hard. "Oh? So when Sly's man, Samson, dug into my bank account and saw all these tiny micro-transactions, it wasn't you keeping tabs on my fortune? It wasn't you making illegal inquiries into my net worth? Huh. That's funny. I'm pretty sure he said he could trace each of those security breaches to you. You were smart enough not to just steal everything, that would have led to direct investigation, and you'd run the risk of getting caught. I mean, you aren't *totally* arrogant. You *are* human. Though, you do think you're better than the majority of computer geeks, otherwise you never would have sent Maeve those threats via email."

Maeve sobbed, her body shaking so hard he could see it from where he was standing. Blaze went to her, helping her to sit in one of the barstools, his comforting hand on her shoulder.

Fuck, AJ wanted to be the one standing beside her, holding her up, comforting her.

But he had to take out the trash first.

"AJ, I have no idea where you get these ideas from. Obviously *that woman* is filling your head with lies. Why would I need to threaten her? She's a fat nobody, she's nothing like me. You and I, we're perfect together. She made all this up to try to get her for yourself. Those emails she sent you as Swan, those were her trying to trick you, scheming to get your personal information so she could blackmail you. I admit, I confronted her when I came that first time. I only claimed to be Swan because I fell in love with what I read— the man…not the money."

Holy shit, the woman was so fucking delusional, he couldn't even keep up with the web of lies she was spinning.

Tall and built like a linebacker, Det. Oliveira strode forward, handcuffs in plain sight in his hand.

Denise grew frantic, backing up as the detective moved forward, her head on a swivel, looking for a way out. Sly and AJ were blocking the entrance, and she would have to get by silent Samson and the detective to get out the back.

She was trapped. By her own lies and the men she'd fucked with.

"You shouldn't have threatened our women," Sly snarled, his face a mask of disgust and rage.

Her hands around her throat, where the invisible noose tightened even more, she shrieked, "No, I—"

"Denise Walters, you are under arrest for—"

"No!" she screamed, fighting against the unsurprisingly strong hold of the detective as he wrapped her wrists in bracelets of steel.

Oliveira continued as if never interrupted. "You have the right to remain silent…."

As the man droned on, Denise finally deflated, the fight leaving her.

Fuck. She deserved every last page of the book being thrown at her.

Needing to be with his woman, he hurried across the room to Maeve, pulling her into his arms.

Great big sobs shook her frame, and he held her, his cheek pressed against the top of her head. Blaze said something to him and moved away, but AJ couldn't focus on that, he could only focus on the woman falling apart in his embrace.

As more police officers entered the building, and Sly, Blaze, and Samson spoke to them in quiet tones, AJ held his woman as she cried.

Finally, the sobbing stopped and she pulled her face from his chest. Peering up at him with wide blue eyes filled with stark relief and burgeoning joy, she croaked, "It's over?"

"Yeah, baby, it's over," he declared, skimming his lips over her cheek. The taste of her tears making his soul groan from the depths of his being. For the rest of his life, he would never make her cry again.

"But how did you figure out what she was doing?"

Shame made his cheeks flame, and he ducked his head in chagrin. "Well…Monday, I was watching you, angry that you'd run from my bed Saturday morning…."

Her cheeks turned red, but she said nothing.

"You got an email and it was like the soul left your body. You turned white, your body sunk in on itself—I could tell that something was wrong. Really wrong. So, after you left, I went home and texted Blaze about getting access to your emails. I wanted to see what you saw that hurt you so much. I wanted to take the look off your face and fix whatever was wrong. What I found…." He shuddered with the memory of it. "She'd threatened the woman I love, and my sister, and my friends. I couldn't just do nothing, Maeve. So, I called Blaze and Sly. We talked and came up with the plan to draw Denise to Jackson Key, lock her out of the White systems and wipe her phone, and then confront and arrest her."

Maeve breathed in deep, her body quaking against his.

"I can't believe it's over, that she can't hurt anyone." She blinked back tears. "Callie and Lexi…." She gritted her teeth at whatever thought crossed her mind, then she said, "Lexi was the one I was most worried about. She's only nine, Denise could have done so much damage, simply by hurting Callie—she didn't even have to directly target Lexi."

"Yeah, but that bitch did. And she deserves to go to hell for that."

"I think twenty-five years in a minimum-security federal prison will have to do," Detective Oliveira drawled as he came to stand beside them, concern for Maeve warming his dark brown eyes.

"Hey man, thanks for coming," AJ said, his appreciation for the man growing. When they'd been introduced, AJ learned that Camilo Oliveira had just transferred in from

LA, where he'd been a homicide detective. Wanting a slower life with less murder, he chose a job where he could capture criminals of the less murder-y variety.

"It was my pleasure, truly," Camilo said, grinning. Turning to AJ and Maeve, he said, "Come by the station in the morning to give your statements,"

Maeve nodded and AJ gave a chin lift.

"Meet up on Thursday, Anchors, I'll buy the first round," Blaze said, offering his hand to the detective.

"You got it."

AJ, his arm around a still trembling Maeve, led her from the building and toward his car.

"Let's get out of here. I need to be alone with you," he murmured against her ear. This time, her trembling was for a different reason. Her blue eyes dilated, her face flushing pink, her perfect lips forming an O.

"Yes, let's go, please," she whimpered, sliding her breasts against him. "You confronting Denise…. That was so hot, I think I might come right here."

He groaned. "Fuck that. That orgasm is mine."

With a happy cry, Maeve took off, running toward AJ's truck, which he'd parked on the far side of the lot.

He didn't hesitate to give chase. He'd follow her no matter where she ran.

chapter
TWENTY-THREE

"Is this really happening?" she murmured into his chest, a sigh of contentment following after.

He chest vibrated with a silent laugh.

After their confrontation with Denise and her arrest, AJ was dragged her from Happy Jack's to his condo, where they made short work of getting naked.

"I must have really pleasured you good if you think you're dreaming, baby."

Giggling, she slapped his chest playfully.

"You know what I mean. After all that's happened...I'm finally here. Where I've always wanted to be."

He kissed her head and moaned softly. "You know it's the same for me, right?"

She snorted. "Uh, no." Impossible. The man hadn't been waiting around for her, he'd been playing the field. She'd seen, with her own eyes, some of the women he'd pick up at at the bars, take home with him, and then date casually until he got bored. They were never her—they hadn't even looked like her. Tall, skinny, gorgeous beach babes. Then there was her, the average, plain, chubby girl who was pining after him.

Apparently, though, now that she knew the truth, he'd been watching her. Seeing her even though she'd been living her life in the shadows. She couldn't believe how incredible it all was.

Alejandro Mendez loved her. Wanted forever with *her*.

He squeezed her, his arms an iron band around her naked body. She melted into him, never wanting to know what space between them felt like.

"Yes, it's the same. I might have fucked a lot of women, but none of them, not a single one of them, ever meant a damn thing to me. I got the pleasure but I was still empty afterward. This, right here with you, was what I've always wanted. This goes beyond sex. This intimacy, this closeness, it's like my soul is touching yours, like my heart is beating with yours. I've never had that with anyone else, Maeve. Only with you. I love you."

Her heart kicked against her sternum and her breath caught. Such beautiful words. Moved by the depth of emotion in his eyes, she lifted her face and pressed a kiss to his waiting mouth.

"Only you," she whispered. "I adore you, Alejandro

Mendez." She kissed him again, their lips opening, their tongues twining with one another. Deepening the kiss, she threaded her fingers through his soft hair, holding him against her as she attacked him with her mouth.

He groaned, taking control, drawing her in then devouring her, until she was dizzy from the lack of oxygen and the need to taste all of him all over again. Her hand sliding from his head to his shoulders where she dug in her nails, her passion for him driving her to drag him closer, to never let him go.

Breaking the kiss, he dropped his forehead to hers and smirked.

"Looks like the mouse has become a tigress as well," he rumbled, flexing his back muscles. His hand on her breast kneaded her plump flesh as his other hand slipped down to grab firm hold of her ass cheek. "Fuck, I love your curves. All this lush sexiness, just for me."

She giggled. Never had she thought a man like AJ would appreciate the extra-ness of her body. But the man couldn't get enough, just like she couldn't get enough of him.

"A tigress, huh? From mouse to vixen to tigress. There's a swan in there somewhere," she teased, joy filling her.

"I never did ask…why SWAN? Why not pick an actual name?" he inquired, his hand drawing sensual circles over the sensitive flesh of her back.

Her skin prickling from his touch, she shivered, making him laugh quietly.

"Well…when I first decided to email you, I…I didn't feel like I had an identity strong enough. You know how I was—hiding behind the computer monitor, sticking to myself, never showing my true self to anyone really. Yeah, I hung out with Sally and Anna, but I still felt like I couldn't let myself be myself around them. Spending years living in the shadow of a vain stepmom and her pretty, mean family, I learned to be seen, then dismissed, then ignored. Next to my family, I felt like a caricature of the ugly family disgrace. Next to Anna and Sally, I felt like the DUFF—the designated, ugly, fat friend."

He pinched her ass and she yelped. "You know that's not fucking true. Fuck your family for being bitches to you. They were jealous and don't deserve a moment of your time and energy. As far as Anna and Sally—those girls would never think of you like that."

She glowered at him, though attempting to stay angry at him when he was looking down at her with such love was impossible. She heaved a sigh and brushed a kiss over the warm, smooth skin of his chest.

"I know that, but that doesn't stop the insecurities," she admitted. Tracing the outline of the sun tattoo over his right pec, she felt his muscles twitch at her touch.

Hmmm....

"She Without A Name became She Who Awakened Need," he quipped, his voice smooth yet thick like warm chocolate. Obviously, all the touching was getting to him.

Good. She wouldn't mind another round of hot sex. He must have been thinking the same thing because his dick grew hard against the thigh she had draped over him. Hard, long, and...*God*...it was pulsing.

Slick drenched her folds, and she fought to keep her mind focused on the conversation.

"Damn, I awaken your need, huh," she purred, her hand splaying over his chest. His heart raced beneath her palm. The pounding matching hers, beat for beat. "What is it that you *need?*"

He chuckled, grabbing her hand to press a kiss into her palm. "The only thing I will ever need is you."

"Hmmmm." She brushed a kiss over his nipple and he tensed. "All you need, huh?"

His breathing stuttered. "Uh huh," he replied. His hand cupping her left breast, his thumb circling her nipple. It was her turn to tense, her body pulling taut like a bow string.

"So…you don't need children…or the house and the picket fence?" What the hell was she saying? Were words coming out of her mouth? She couldn't focus, her mouth was moving on its own, and she didn't care what was coming out of it.

He thrust up, rolling Maeve over on her back until he was braced over her, his bulging biceps holding his massive body in place over her. She spread her thighs, cradling his naked erection against her wet heat. She raised her hips, curling into him, begging for him. He ground against her, making her cry out.

"You want babies, I'll plant my seed so far inside you, you'll be pregnant within the week. You want the picket fence, I'll draw up the designs tomorrow and build our dream house right up the beach from Sally and Sly. You want the world, baby, and I will wrap it in a bow for you. There is nothing I need more than to give you everything you have ever hoped or dreamed for."

Overcome at his words, tears slipped from her eyes and down her cheeks.

"God, I love you," she exclaimed, her throat tight.

EVE BLACK

His eyes, so intense, so filled with love, so green and bright and glimmering with joy, peered down at her.

"I love you. Forever," he declared before taking her mouth in a kiss that stole her breath.

Before she lost all ability to think, she pictured them, together, standing in the sunlight, their arms around each other, their hearts beating for one another…far away from the shadows.

epilogue

Callie Williams tugged her purse strap high across her chest, and squared her shoulders. She was going to march right into that bank, look the loan officer in the eye, and tell him exactly why she deserved a small business loan. She had the business plan—which she'd been working on for the last four years, day and night, until her hair fell out—in her professional looking leather briefcase. Her usual messy mop of copper curls was straightened and pinned back into a sophisticated bun to the point of pain, and her makeup was clean and understated. Thank heavens her best friend Maeve's sex-goddess friend, Sally, had been on hand to throw out the five-year-old Dollar

Store eyeshadow—which Callie had bought back when she'd actually given a flying squirrel if she looked good—before Callie made herself look like a killer clown. Her not so svelte, post-baby, currently-carbs-are-life body had been another issue she'd needed help covering. She was lumpy in all the wrong places, and she could definitely use a little more sun. Pale and plump. Not a good combination. She was wearing her most professional get up, care of Sally's closet—thigh-hugging black pencil skirt, frilly cream-colored button-up silk blouse, and sky-high heels that Maeve said made her legs look "killer". She'd much rather be wearing loose, worn jeans, a worn-in t-shirt three sizes too big, and her shit-kickers, but if she showed up to her appointment looking like a homeless country bumpkin, Mr. Wells, managing loan officer of Jackson Key Bank, would turn her out on her ear before she even said a word.

The meeting with Mr. Wells lasted for thirty minutes, and Callie left his office feeling a little less anxious than when she went in.

She could do this.

Her phone pinged.

Maeve: Did you get the loan?

Callie: Don't know yet. He has to go over the business plan.

Maeve: Did he seem hopeful?

Callie: He did, but i'm not going to get my hopes up.

Maeve: Why not? Also, don't you think it's weird that we spell out all our words and use proper punctuation...even in texts?

Callie giggled, loving her friend to pieces for her inexplicable ability to lighten any mood. Callie needed that now more than ever. Her future was now in the hands of a pot-bellied man with a bad comb over.

This was her one chance to make something of herself... something her daughter would be proud of. Something *she* could be proud of. It didn't hurt that she'd be a business owner and finally get off state welfare, which had been a goal since she'd first gotten that blessing and curse of an EBT card.

No, she wasn't ashamed of being on food stamps—it kept her daughter fed, but she didn't want to rely on the hard-earned money of others to support her small family. Lord knows Lexi's father would never send a dime of money—and she wouldn't take it now if he did. She didn't need him now. She'd needed him ten years ago when she was a newly graduated eighteen-year-old, struggling to come to terms with a tectonic shift in her axis.

Lexi's father had been a twenty-three-year-old with a dazzling smile and drool-worthy body, who'd come in to her beachside town to celebrate being drafted into the NFL. He'd said he'd graduated college early and was taking advantage of the time off before training began in the late summer. They'd met a bonfire. For her, it had been love at first sight.

He'd been her first kiss, her first love, her first...everything. She'd handed herself over to him with the wistful romantic hopefulness of a naïve virgin. Too young and inexperienced to see the truth hiding in plain sight.

There were flags everywhere.

He never introduced her to his friends, never called her—only texted, and he never talked about his family. They'd spent three months meeting in secret. Not even her family knew about her clandestine love affair with the sexy, older man. It was forbidden, which made it all the more incredible. She'd foolishly thought they'd been falling in love, happily planning a future together, where she'd attend the University of Florida since she'd earned a full ride there, and he'd play for New York. Eventually, she'd follow him once she finished her degree in English Literature. She was so in love, she just *knew* they could survive a long-distance relationship. They were meant to be.

He hadn't agreed.

It had all been a lie.

She groaned, hating how stupid and foolish eighteen-year-old Calliope Williams had been. Twenty-eight-year-old Callie Williams, single mother, had to get that loan. She couldn't depend on anyone else to make her dreams come true.

Cheers & chapters, a combination wine tasting room and bookstore, was her dream.

Callie: No. We're too cool for abbreviations and silly emojis.

Maeve: I think it makes us the least cool people we know.

She smiled down at her phone and opened the door, hurrying out and into the now blistering afternoon sun.

"Oomph!" she grunted as she slammed into a wall that smelled of cloves and sun tan lotion. "Goodness, I'm sorry," she blubbered, pushing the hair that had come loose from her bun out of her eyes.

Dang her and her inability to multitask.

"No need to apologize…."

She jerked and looked up…and her heart stopped.

Taller than her five-foot-five by a good foot, with shoulders as wide as a doorway, the man before her was quite possibly the most gorgeous man she'd ever seen. Bright eyes as glittering and blue as the Caribbean Sea, a smirk that showed off a straight white smile and two sexy dimples. His dark hair was cropped close to his head, which only seemed to emphasize the startling symmetry of his beautiful face.

A face she hadn't seen in ten years.

Ethan Brass. Ten years older. Ten years bigger and handsomer. Ten years harder and more filled out. Ten years richer and fancier, with his designer jeans that fit over his thick thigh muscles, and his tight designer t-shirt that stretched over his well-defined, bulging biceps and sculpted pecs, and snuggled up against his narrow waist and hips, highlighting the cut abdominal muscles flexing beneath.

Lord 'a' mercy.

It had been ten years since the man before her had told her he loved her, promised her the world, offered her everything she ever wanted on a platter. Then he ripped out her heart and stomped on it, a grin on his face for her trouble.

Oh no. Oh no, no, no!

He flinched, his sexy as all heck smirk slipping a little bit. Shoot, she must've said that out loud. Then again, she didn't give a cat's whiskers if the man heard her muttering her shock and displeasure under her breath. He deserved to know his presence was unwanted. Actually, he deserved much more than that. Like a swift kick in the pants.

Too bad she didn't have the time nor inclination to stand around letting all that old hate and hurt to surface.

"Hello, Calliope."

Her name in his mouth was like a curse falling from

pretty, poisonous lips. He had no right to put her name in his lying, cheating mouth.

"Keep my name out of your mouth," she sneered, the collar on her dress shirt feeling awfully tight all of a sudden. "You don't have the right to speak my name nor to me."

Ethan didn't seem moved by her vitriol, only pinning her with a stare that said nothing. Raising his ham sized fist, he flattened it and reached out to her as if to touch her.

She took a big step back. He would never touch her again.

Not like any man has touched you since him anyway, she mentally snarked. Not that she hadn't tried, but being a fulltime mom and working to keep a roof over their heads with only a high school and then junior college education, she had little time for romance or bed acrobatics. There had been a few men who'd tempted her into first and second dates, but none of them had lit that spark inside her that told her he would be worth the risk.

Only one man had ever done that, and that risk had been too high a price to pay.

Ethan reached out again, his hand stopping before he could touch her, his fingers curling into his palm…like he wanted to touch her, but he was stopping himself.

She took another step back, her gaze never leaving his cursed, gorgeous face.

Why aren't you stepping right over to your car and getting the heck out of here?

Curiosity. Plain and simple. She wanted to know why he was there, and what the heck he thought he could say to her after all these years. Yeah, she was asking for trouble… but she was also deserving of some damn answers.

adoring ALEJANDRO

Answers? He said he loved you, lied to you, then cheated on you when you needed him the most.

"It's good to see you, Callie," he drawled, his deep voice deeper and smoother and sexier than she remembered. But it still had the power to light up her insides like daylight LEDs. "It's been a long time."

"You don't say," she snapped without thinking.

The man had the audacity to grin at her, like he hadn't done her dirty then gone on to earn millions while she and their daughter lived off of ramen noodles, canned tuna, and misfit fruits and vegetables.

Angrier than she'd been in—*you guessed it*—ten years, she hissed at him like a cornered cat.

"Come on, Callie, don't be like that," he pleaded, his voice soft and coaxing, like he was trying to get her to lay on her back so he could stroke her belly.

Or stab her in the heart.

"Shove it up your ass, Brass!" she growled, raised both hands to flip him a double bird, then turned on her heels and strode away. The curse word slipped from her mouth with ease…but she'd pray for forgiveness later. The word fit the predicament.

Hurrying to her lime green, two door hatchback, she opened the door, jumped in, and turned the key in the ignition. Thankfully, the twenty-year-old beater car didn't kick it in that moment because she needed to be as far away from that man as she could get.

She backed out of her parking spot, shifted into drive, then practically burned rubber from the bank parking lot—not once looking back in his direction. She wouldn't give him the satisfaction of another millisecond of her attention.

Pulling onto the four-lane highway that acted as Jackson

Key's main drag, she let heaving breaths she been holding in finally escape. Yep. She was hyperventilating. Maybe she was having a panic attack. Maybe she'd had one in the bank and had hallucinated that whole confrontation on the sidewalk, and she would snap out of it and it would have all been a waking nightmare.

Her brain disagreed with her, flooding her with too many details for it too have been a figment of her imagination.

The sight of Ethan…the heat radiating from his huge, hard body…the scent of him that still lingered in her nose…and the timbre of his voice as it sent shock waves of long dead desire through her blood.

It had been all too real.

She had no idea what the hades Ethan Brass was doing in Jackson Key, but she was determined to avoid him for as long as possible. The town wasn't all that big, but she had no plans to go much of anywhere besides work and the apartment she and Lexi shared with Maeve.

No. There was no reason to assume she'd run into Ethan Brass again. She'd hide out until he left town—because that's what he did, leave.

How hard could it be to avoid the man who'd broken her heart then abandoned her and their daughter? It wasn't like he didn't have a life to get back to in New York, right? It wasn't like Ethan Brass was in town to take up where he left off ten years ago. That was insane. There was no possible way that NFL MVP Ethan Brass was there for a second chance.

Coming Next

Chasing Callie: A Second Chance Romance—
Falling Down #4
Coming 2023

Want to know why Callie is losing her mind, and what Ethan Brass is doing in Jackson Key?

Coming Soon

A whole new world of wolf shifters….
When an alpha rejects his mate, fate intervenes….
And reclaiming their fierce females will take everything they have.

The Sixteenth Moon—Rejected & Reclaimed #1
A Rejected Mates Romance
Coming December 9th 2022

also by
EVE BLACK

Sexy Romance with Curves—Eve writes sexy romance featuring plus-sized heroines and the sexy heroes who fall for them. Because ***Curvy Girls Need Love, Too***!

Contemporary Billionaire Romance

Diamond Bridal Agency Series

Billionaire Bachelor: Michael
Billionaire Bachelor: Vitali
Billionaire Bachelor: Omar

Manhattan Magic Series

Unexpected: A Billionaire Baby Daddy Romance

Contemporary Bad Boy Romance

Cocky Hero Club Series

Down 'n' Dirty Dog

Savage Raiders MC Series

Savage King
Savage Guardian (Coming Fall 2022)

Contemporary Small Town Romance

Falling Down Series

Breaking Blaze: A Best Friends-to-Lovers Romance
Seducing Sallina: A Fling-to-Forever Romance
Adoring Alejandro: An Unrequited Love Romance
Chasing Callie: A Second Chance Romance (Coming 2023)

Paranormal Romance

Rejected & Reclaimed Series

The Sixteenth Moon
(Coming Dec. 9th, 2022)

acknowledgements

This is another of those times where I get to brag about the people who helped me make this book worth reading.

Once again, I must thank **Angela Haddon** for creating a cover that is perfectly *Adoring Alejandro*. I tell her what I'm thinking, and she fashions my thoughts into cover design awesomeness.

I also want to thank **Stacey Blake**, the formatter from heaven. She always shapes my Word doc into eye-catching art.

I know it's weird, but I'd like to thank **my hematologist**. She diagnosed my chronic anemia, which allows me to get the treatment I need to have a fully functioning brain. Let me tell you, trying to write a book with only $1/4^{th}$ a brain is haaaaaard.

To those who buy and read my books—thank you.

To those who engage with me online, and make my day—thank you.

To those who review my books—thank you, thank you, thank you!

Finally, I'd like to acknowledge the woman who introduced me to books. My mother, **Donna**. Thank you, Mom, for being willing to let my bookworm, adolescent person drag you across town on the city bus to the library so that I could indulge in the one thing that helped me escape a world I didn't understand. Thank you for talking books with me, encouraging me to be the author I am, and being my biggest fan. I love you, Mom.

about the
AUTHOR

Eve Black is the sexy contemporary romance-loving alter-ego of a sweet historical romance author…who also writes dark, sexy medieval romance under another name. Eve is one of several personalities in one crazy package. When Eve isn't writing books, she is editing other people's books, or wrangling her children. For fun, Eve loves to read sexy contemporary, paranormal, and historical romance books, binge-watch old TV shows on Netflix, and play mind-numbing games on her tablet.

Eve lives in an untidy house on a little over an acre in rural Northeast Pennsylvania with her husband of 17 years and their four children, two cats, and one chicken.

Find Eve Online:

Website | Newsletter | Facebook | Amazon
Goodreads | Bookbub | Instagram

Eve Black